Black Town

Cries in the Cotton

Michael K. Piper

© **Copyright 2023 - All rights reserved.**

The content contained within this book may not be reproduced, duplicated or transmitted without direct written permission from the author or the publisher.

Under no circumstances will any blame or legal responsibility be held against the publisher, or author, for any damages, reparation, or monetary loss due to the information contained within this book, either directly or indirectly.

Legal Notice:

This book is copyright protected. It is only for personal use. You cannot amend, distribute, sell, use, quote or paraphrase any part, or the content within this book, without the consent of the author or publisher.

Disclaimer Notice:

Please note the information contained within this document is for educational and entertainment purposes only. All effort has been executed to present accurate, up to date, reliable, complete information. No warranties of any kind are declared or implied. Readers acknowledge that the author is not engaged in the rendering of legal, financial, medical or professional advice. The content within this book has been derived from various sources. Please consult a licensed professional before attempting any techniques outlined in this book.

By reading this document, the reader agrees that under no circumstances is the author responsible for any losses, direct or indirect, that are incurred as a result of the use of the information contained within this document, including, but not limited to, errors, omissions, or inaccuracies.

Table of Contents

PROLOGUE 1

CHAPTER 1: THE ROAD FROM THIS TOWN TO THE NEXT 7

CHAPTER 2: COTTON FIELDS MAKE FOR UNLIKELY FRIENDSHIPS 29

CHAPTER 3: GUILTY UNTIL PROVEN INNOCENT 49

CHAPTER 4: ROTTEN SEEDS STILL GROW 69

CHAPTER 5: WHAT DID HE SEE? 89

CHAPTER 6: RUN, WILLY, RUN 111

CHAPTER 7: THE CALM AFTER THE STORM 131

CHAPTER 8: HIDE AND SEEK 149

CHAPTER 9: MEMORIES DISGUISED AS NIGHTMARES 171

CHAPTER 10: THE TRUTH WE TELL 187

EPILOGUE 207

Prologue

It was the kind of heat that stuck to your skin. It didn't sit on you like dry heat, heavy and crushing but avoidable. Rather it was in you, on you and there was simply no way around it.

This sort of heat could make even the strongest of men faint in the fields from its sheer intensity.

It reminds her of her youth, when every emotion was heightened simply 'cause of the heat. You can taste your happiness like sweet tea, anger like bitter olives, and sadness like lemonade.

Perhaps it was appropriate, how hot it was. Funerals in the heat were sometimes easier than those in the rain. It reminded you of sticky summer and childhood, not pain and hardship. Rain had a way of making everything seem bleak and drawing you closer to the heartbreak of passing.

It was a small church with few embellishments. White walls, small windows. A handmade cross hung up on the wall. No gold, no stained glass windows, no lavish art to praise the Lord. Just honest walls that called to honest people to find spirituality, not in the objects, but in the air around them. Perfumed by the people who walked through.

The church was a lot like the deceased, lying peacefully in the casket.

A woman sat in the pews, currently the only attendee of the quiet viewing. Many had come in the morning, others would come in the evening. But the midday heat had pushed people away. Kept them in the cool of their homes where they could sip sweet tea and pretend that the pulsing sun was nothing but a bad dream.

The woman could not leave the church. She had been there all morning, and still she sat, saying a lengthy goodbye. She was unable to properly form words. So much to say and yet none of it felt right.

The black dress clung elegantly to her frame, leaving one thinking she was of higher social class than she was. It had been handled with care throughout her life. When you have less, you touch everything with the most tender of hands. Her ebony skin had weathered. Worn with age and a life of manual labor, she was still as beautiful as she had been as a young woman.

Footsteps can be heard on the wooden floor before a voice announces their presence.

"Hot one today, isn't it?" She turns to look at the man, smiling softly at him. He takes a seat next to her, adjusting the jacket of his suit. His soft blue eyes were taking in the church with curiosity and the slightest tinge of discomfort. He was out of his usual element.

"Indeed it is," she said, her voice soft but firm. The kind of voice you only get with age.

"Were you close to him?" He gestures at the simple wooden box placed in the front of the room.

"Yea," she smiled, memories glinting softly in her eyes like sunlight on a lake. "My days will be a little darker without him in it."

A silence befalls them as they savor the remembrance of a person once so vibrant and full of life and now is not. Strange how people slip from us, something so concrete in its thoughts and feelings just ceases to exist.

"Did ya know 'em?" She asks the stranger, trying to equate his frayed features to someone younger. Someone she may have known or even loved.

"Only a little," was his response. She nodded, her eyes turning back to the front, giving him a break from her inquisitive looks.

"One of the good ones," she said, tears gathering around her words making them sound slightly slurred. "But Lord knows that good people suffer the greatest hardships."

"What do you mean?" The gentleman asked her, curious to the soft folk tale allure of her voice. The promise of a story, tinged in the glasses of the past but dipped in truth pure and intense.

"Everyone has a story, some are more terrible and

greater than others." The allure of her voice was fading but the gentleman didn't want it to. He wanted to hear the story and understand the person he had wondered about for years.

"That they do," he nodded. "I am afraid that I do not know theirs." He tipped his head respectfully to the deceased, his words hinting at his need to know more. A need that burned within him for a desperate reason. One that he would not reveal too soon. After all, he did not know the woman he was speaking to. Better to hush up.

"A real pity. There is much to be learned from that story."

"Would you tell it to me?" He decides that being direct with her is the only way to get any real information out of the woman. She is the kind that can weave a fiddle out of cotton.

"Oh, it's a long story." She brushes off, smiling softly at him. "Far too long for us to get through in a cotton pickin' minute."

He paused for a second before speaking "I have the time. You know how it is when you get old, far too much time on your hands and nothing much to do."

She laughed at his words, the sound deep with life and warm with a tenderness that only comes when you truly care about the world.

"Still, it's not a happy story, it will be one that will leave the taste of char in your mouth. We should be celebrating a life with better stories, not the ones that shift the axis of the world. Those are better told when the weather is colder and the dead are as close as the wind."

He pondered what she said for a minute. He supposed she was right. But wasn't this story a great one? Shouldn't it be told in his last moments still connected to the world? Before the grave grew with mildew, words worn away with rain and the world forgot. People move on quickly if you let them.

"You said it was a great story?" he questioned.

"It is."

"Then should it not be one which is celebrated and passed on? Even the hard stories should be told, there are lessons to be learned."

She sighs a little before she begins, "I must inform you, I was a mere bystander to the proceedings and it happened so long ago that some of my memories are foggy." The gentleman was watching her now, attentive as she spoke. He nodded for her to continue. All the best stories were smoothed over by the passing of time. It was the slight creative liberties that made them compelling, even if it meant the truth was a little different.

"The story begins in the winter of my twelfth year…"

Chapter 1:

The Road From This Town to the Next

I remember that winter better than most of the winters of my youth. Something about it was cutting, icy in a way we weren't used to. But looking back has its faults, a funny way of memory over exaggerating and under exaggerating everything, and so I can't be sure of how cold it really was.

Perhaps it was most frosted in memory due to the sheer intensity of the summer that followed, one that scorched and burned everything around it. The sun was so hot and unforgiving that it baked the ground into a hard clay that was simply unworkable.

Still, I remember that cold as much as you remember your own face. How my fingers and toes ached with each waking. My room was not fitted for such weather' It was icy as it let wind in in all the wrong places and Mama never could afford the warmer blankets, the ones that trapped the heat in rather than letting your body heat desperately try to warm up that little room until you were too cold to move.

The cold was never good for the plantations. Too cold and you suffered a frost so bad that nothing would be able to grow but not cold enough and the summer would become unbearable as the heat of July raged the worst sort of war. Heat was worse for the plantations. You could work in the cold. The numbness was bearable when you focused on the repetitive task of working on the cotton plants. But heat was deadly to the sharecroppers. If it was too hot then you simply couldn't work and not working meant no money.

I remember my mornings of the winter. It was far too cold to sleep but I would come back into awareness as the sky turned that lifeless winter gray with a sun too weak to really bring any color back to life. I would throw the blankets from my body and shuffle out of my small room, trying to remove the pins and needle coldness from my bones.

Mama was always in the main living area preparing breakfast. That sludgy porridge that tastes like sawdust. But scavenging simply wasn't possible in the cold. Everything died, and there was little coin to spare when you were months away from harvest. I was a child of Black Town. We know not to complain.

My job was cleaning. Mama said I was good at it but I didn't want to be good at cleaning. I wanted to be good at reading, arithmetic, and all the other things I learned at school. You couldn't do much with cleaning but you could do a lot with school.

Still, I hushed up about my dreams around Mama and Father. They would turn gray with their inability to deliver me the world I so desperately wanted. It was hard for them, knowing I would never live and learn as I deserved. Emotions were easily twisted into anger. My parents' frustration passed swiftly. It rained down like a sheet of water and then it was over. No matter how quick, it was better not to anger them.

The talk of the future was for the people who had money to buy them time.

I plunged my hands into the icy water in the basin, using that threadbare sponge to scrub off the remains of last night's dinner. The cold meant we had to leave the plates soaking overnight before the sticky bits would peel away from the enamel.

Sometimes the water was so cold that my skin would crack and peel. I would spend the day trying to warm my hands up. I couldn't get my clothes messy.

Once I finished with the plates and pots I would eat the porridge, shoveling heavy spoonfuls into my mouth, uninterested in the taste but grateful for the food. Saw dust was better than nothing, especially when the days were short and the nights long. At least my belly wouldn't ache from hunger.

After that, Mama combed my hair with calloused hands that tugged and pulled too hard. I bit the discomfort down with watery eyes and a tight grip on my skirt. Looking neat was important. I was a representation of my parents and no Johnson would ever look unruly and untamed. An iron fist was used to control children. My hair was included in that equation it seemed.

It wasn't long before my Mama was pushing me out of the house and urging me to hurry to school.

"Don't be late now," she would say, her tone a warning-love.

"Yes ma'am," I would nod and begin the long walk to school.

My Mama was the best mama there ever was. Her body was perfect for carrying and providing for children. Wide hips, a broad chest, and plush body that gave the best hugs.

I remember her as the most warm and loving figure in my life, as well as the most strict. She could comfort you after injury like no one else. Her arms were a safe, warm place that I could rush into and be provided with everything I needed to make the world right again. But I also remember that, of my parents, she had been in charge of my punishments.

Mama's hands were strong and worn with the physical labor she had spent her entire life doing. They were perfect for whipping even my most wandering strands of hair into shape and keeping her unruly children in line.

Mama knew what I needed and how best to give it to me, even if it was difficult to hear or experience. She knew how to love. She, better than anyone, knew that love was a careful balance of care and command.

My father was the more aloof of my parents. He had dedicated his entire life to the cotton plantations and sometimes providing for his family came before his family.

He was a big man, bigger than most of the people in Black Town. Tall and broad, he was an immovable force. He worked long hours, often gone before I woke and back after I fell asleep. But he had always been the one to give me my baths and was a source of wisdom and knowledge.

When I had first begun to ask questions, I had asked all of them to my father. He had been the only one with the answers and he always delivered, never tiring of my ceaseless wonder.

He was distant from his children, less inclined to coddle and cuddle us. Of the few joyful memories I had with him I remember how he would play with us, running wild with me until I ran out of energy and then carrying my sleepy frame home in his strong arms.

We lived on the Pickney Plantation. A white family who had a sharecropping agreement with my father. They were good people, but they knit closely to those that stood where they stood. Respectful of Black Town but not overly fond.

We lived in the fields. My family was dedicated to their work. We needed to step out to work the minute we woke, so the walk from town to the cotton fields placed a burden on that ability. We lived with the fields at our doorstep and the pressing embrace of work squeezing us tight.

Our home was made of brick and tin. A little on the small side. We cooked and ate our meals in the same room and bathed in the kitchen as well. My parents shared a room with my brother and I slept in what had once been a storage area of the house. But my unexpected arrival had called for a change in the space.

I would always arrive at the schoolhouse far too early. Mama worked early as well and could not afford to be minding me during the day. If I was at the school house then she knew I couldn't get into trouble, at least for a couple of hours.

As the sky started to tinge a pale gray-yellow, I would sit on the step by the door waiting for Miss Stevens to arrive. She used to get there a little before school started but after she found me sitting and waiting she would try to get there earlier and let me in. Especially in winter.

"Can't be sitting out here in the cold," she would mutter as she unlocked the door, looking down at me next to her. It was only a little warmer inside the room but at least there were chairs.

The school house was somewhat of a box that had come together slowly with the odd donation and help from the Town. When it was first built, it didn't even have a proper floor, let alone tables and chairs. The walls were still blank but there was somewhat of a floor and at least we had chairs we could sit on.

In the beginning of the year there were often so many children that the room was crowded and the tables and chairs were removed to make space for all of us. But by the time mid winter rolled around there was only a handful of us left. School was a luxury that resulted in less helping hands to feed hungry mouths.

There wasn't much to Black Town. Dirt roads, a general store run by the Pitchers, and one or two little homes for the people who didn't work on the plantations. People like Miss Stevens.

It was nothing like the splendor and vastness of Roswell and Father had told me that Roswell was small in comparison to the cities. I had never been to the city before but I dreamed of it. I dreamed of the opportunity to run away from the life I lived here. To study at the place called college, so that I could get a job. A real job. Not cotton picking.

The sunrise was slow. In the summer it was brilliant and violent. Such intensity in the way that it displaced the sky's blue that I didn't know enough words to describe it all. As the gray turned to a milky yellow and eventually a washed-out blue, I felt a sigh on my lips. Hopefully summer would come quickly and there would be life once more. Every season, I worried that I had seen the last of it.

Miss Stevens arrived early like always and I followed her inside. Some days, I would ask her all the questions that jumbled in my mind. That prayed on my tongue for hours until I found someone who could answer them. But Miss Stevens was beginning to struggle with them too. She had been a perfect source of knowledge in the beginning but she was starting to wilt and buckle under the weight of my thirst.

"I don't know," she would say, her eyes understanding the burning need in me to have them answered and heartbroken that she wasn't able to meet the challenge. She may have been educated, but even she had limits to her knowledge.

So most of my time in class was spent waiting for it to end. I desperately wanted to learn but the things that were taught were repetitive and boring. I knew how to read, I knew how to write and I knew my time's tables. I would stare out the small window in the corner of the room with only a strip of sky visible. Sometimes I could see a bird soar for a moment and I would push down the desperation to join it in the sky.

Eventually, the school day would come to an end and I would trudge along the road, through Black Town, kicking my feet as I dragged myself toward Roswell where work awaited me.

A year ago I had been free to do as I pleased after school. The only rule being that I had to be back by sunset. When I was a lot younger I used to play with the other children. The cotton fields would transform themselves into oceans, castles, and other fantastical lands we could dream of.

We played roughly and loudly, messing up our clothes, lining our cheeks with dirt. The world was a vast and open place, one that we could make our own no matter who we were. We were candles burning brightly, unaware of the importance of wax.

I liked the play, it gave me control over the other children. I was quick to think of new games and plots, they hung on to my every word. Waiting. It didn't matter that I was smaller and younger than most of them. Knowledge, or lack thereof, is how you hold people hostage.

But as I grew, I learnt about something a little bit more powerful than play. Something that helped me to answer all the burning questions in my head. Put the world into perspective. I learnt to listen.

A child is nothing much to most older folk. Just a bundle of over-excited energy, too much noise and not enough muscle to be useful. They talk over us, look around us and never really understand how sharp our minds are.

It used to confuse me greatly, weren't they once a child just like me?

But growing up is a whole lot of forgetting and very little understanding.

Mama and Father would talk about things in front of me that they would never say in front of Big Willy. Too many words I didn't understand, things that would only confuse me.

"Not in front of her" Mama would say, trying to push father out of the house. A conversation dipped in gray from the simplicity of a child's mind.

"She doesn't understand a word we are saying" he would grumble.

He was right, I didn't. But I also didn't know how to listen yet. How to peel understanding from a lifted brow or the turn of a lip. I would get there. The more I listened the more things started to clear. The world's pieces shift together and burn brilliantly.

I would learn, too, how to hide between the fabric of the two worlds. The one where I was old enough to understand therefore unable to sit in and listen without consequences. And the world where I was still too young, innocent, naive. I walked the fine line with the expertise of tightrope walking. Knowing what would come if I tilted too far to the one side.

I hid understanding behind long blinks and disinterested smiles. I would hint at how much I knew in how I moved, how I swept through situations with a greater understanding of how the cogs connected. But I was quick to dismiss the claims of understanding.

"I don't know Ma." I would wave away as I ran to play with the other children. Her eyes watched me carefully, trying to pinpoint how much was a lie in the flick of my skirt.

"She's so clever but she doesn't know nothin' about any of the important stuff," Is what the older men of Black Town would say when they thought I wasn't listening. My back pressed tightly to the wall and my breath holding so they wouldn't know I was still there.

"Book smarts mean nothin' in a world where you gotta fight dirty just to stand," another would say. I could hear the shake of his head in how his words carried on the wind.

As a child, intelligence is only valuable so long as no one knows you have it. You have to keep information tight to your chest like a secret.

But still, the world I lived in was narrow and small. It didn't hold much apart from the fields, my little bedroom and the town center that wasn't much of a town. It was spring of that year that it would be opened up, I would begin to see the world as more than the fields of my home. I would hunger for this new world, dipped in possibility and violent in its promise for more.

"It's about time you start working girl," Mama said one morning as she yanked my hair into submission.

"Yes ma'am." I said. I hadn't understood what she meant but assumed that it would be in the fields like Willy. Her next words would puzzle me until I made my way to a neat porch painted in white.

"You are to go straight to Roswell after school," she began with her instructions. "Ask one of them folk around the town where Mrs. Fields house is. When you get to the door, you knock promptly three times and introduce yourself as Hattie Mae's girl. Got it?" She had said, turning me around so I could look her in the eye as I committed to her commands.

"Yes Ma'am," I had uttered, not sure of why I was being sent to Roswell. What work could await me in some old woman's home? Still I feared the wrath of my mother more than the uncertainty that sat heavy in the pit of my gut.

Roswell was not anything I had ever expected nor wanted. It was a strange town filled with strange folk. It was large in comparison to Black Town. The streets were named and there were many of them lined back to back making little squares that you could walk in circles around. The houses were colorful and edged in a pretty white. They could afford to be decorative and picky.

It felt easy to get trapped there, especially on the main street that was filled with stores and other buildings I had yet to learn the names for. There were a lot of people, all in such a small amount of space. I remember spinning around endlessly, wondering if I would get lost in all the faces around me.

The shops had large clean windows that you could see inside with advertisements sprayed on in bright colors to invite you in. Colorful dresses more beautiful than anything I had imagined, a hardware with tools glittering silver in the display and a grocery with the brightest fruits I had ever seen. It all looked so intense and a little overwhelming.

I was taking in the sights around me, spinning to orientate myself and find something that could hint to where it was that I needed to go. How do you find one house in a sea of them?

I start walking down what I could guess is the main road, looking at the shops and everything that they sell while trying to keep an eye out for someone that might be friendly enough to help me if I were to ask. Mostly the people seem to be rushing from this place to the next, like they do not have enough hours in the day to get all their important business done.

As I was taking a look at an assortment of sweets displayed in the window of one shop, I accidentally bumped into a man. I took a few steps back and bow my head in greeting.

"My apologies, I didn't see you there, Sir." I quickly said not wanting to be seen as disrespectful or impolite. When I look up to meet his eyes, it was to see his lips curling back over his teeth like a feral animal. Anger and disgust are emotions clearly expressed on his face but the latter is new to me. I have never seen such an emotion cross someone's face and know that it is directed at me.

He reared back as he realized I was making eye contact with him and then spat at my feet.

"Negro scum," he sneered and then stomped away from me, as if being in my presence for a second too long would infect him.

Frozen, I stood there unsure of what to do. I had bumped into him but I didn't expect it to warrant a reaction such as that. To have my race called out straight to my face with utter disgust and anger had me shrink into myself.

My shoulders slumped and a newfound panic gripped me. I had started to look for someone to give me directions. Surely Mrs. Fields would be better if Mama was sending me to her. Still, that river of fear trickled through me. What if she was just as hateful and spat at me the second I walked through.

The town of wonder and shiny things was quickly turning dark and muddy. I made sure not to bump into anyone else as I walked past the shops, my eyes now glued to the ground.

It had taken a while before I found someone I was brave enough to ask for directions. He was a man the same shade as me and his eyes looked kind. He was sitting outside of a store. I didn't know what it sold but the door looked expensive. In his hands were cups of thick, black polish—the kind Mama would make me clean my shoes with—that I know stained your hands when you touched it, leaving a sticky, mucky residue over your fingers and nails.

"Mister, Mister!" I call out to him, tipping my head in respect as I stepped toward him.

"Yes little Miss?" He asked, his eyes kind like my fathers but without all the anger in between.

"Do ya happen to know where Mrs. Fields lives?" I ask him as politely as I could, my hands behind my back as I rock onto my toes. Nerves were filling me to the very brim.

"Ah," he says, pausing to think for a minute, "The old gossip lives on the northside of town."

He keeps talking, giving me directions that I repeat in my head over and over so I don't forget them. Trying to understand how I am going to navigate such unfamiliar territory while still being on time. I am sure that Mrs. Fields is waiting for me and I don't want to keep her waiting for long. It would be impolite.

"Hurry along now," he encouraged, showing me away with his hands.

"Yessir, thank you," I smiled back and then quickly began to walk the direction he pointed. He had said the house was bright orange, that I couldn't miss it if I tried and it made a wave of relief slip smoothly through me.

I did manage to find it. The house was right at the edge of the town, a bright orange one that neared on an eyesore with a pretty white porch wrapping around the building. It was verging on looking old, with a wild, overgrown garden in the front that had it been summer, would have been filled with wild flowers and grass so high it would attract rats. It felt cared for, but in a careless sort of way.

I hop between the stones, careful to not touch the yellowing grass and then walk up the stairs. They creak and groan underneath me. The sound makes me wince as I reach up and knock on the old wooden door.

It takes a moment but the door is pulled open and I am met by an older woman. She is still beautiful and her clothes are lavish but her face is beginning to wane in its beauty. The skin is crumpling and sagging in places.

"Good Afternoon Missus. I am Hattie Mae's daughter. She sent me to you." I keep my eyes down and respectful, unaware of how she looks me up and down. The narrowing of her lids.

"Yes I know," she says, her voice sharp. "And look up too, child! Always meet people head on, no matter who they are."

I lift my head and meet her eyes as she steps away from the door.

The woman before me was not at all who I expected. Mrs. Fields was not a young woman. She was very far from it. Her hair was an almost blinding sliver that shimmered with her movements, making it almost seem alive. But she had not been the old woman hunched over with a cane that I saw in my head when Mama had told me about her.

She was beautiful in many ways but her face had been weathered by her many years of life and she had lost the lushness of youth. Her features were striking. It was something I discovered not just in my first meeting with her but in the many hours I would spend in her home.

Her eyes were a watery gray that I assumed had once been a bright blue but had waned with her experience and growth. Her clothes were lavish and far more stylish than most of the women her age I would come to meet. She dressed in dark tones such as blacks, dark blues, and browns often. I don't think I ever saw her in any bright colors the entire time I knew her.

When I had first met her, standing outside her door and raising my head to meet her eyes, I realized that she was everything I aspired to be in my life. Her dark blue dress made her look respectable while still holding gorgeously onto her frame and her lips had a deep blush tone to them. A color so unnatural and unreal to me that I would develop an obsession with it as a young woman.

Best of all to my younger self was that she radiated a sense of knowledge and pride. I felt that perhaps, just maybe, I had found the person to answer all my questions.

"Hurry, come in," she scolds and gestures for me to close the door behind me as I step carefully onto the carpeted floors. I follow behind her as she walks to a room and then takes a seat in a plush chair with pretty pink flowers covering it. Nothing in a room really seems to match. An odd collection of bits and bobs that have no connection to each other. Somehow the chaos of the room makes it feel put together.

I stand at the door, waiting for an instruction to come in and not daring to step in further than the threshold. This is her home and as the help I am not meant to be seen.

"I don't know what your mother was thinking," she says as she drops into the chair, her hands flaring out in a manner that can only be described as ridiculous. "Sending a child to do an adults work. You should be in school or playing with the other children."

I wanted to respond but I couldn't be seen as talking back so I just kept quiet and listened to her speak.

"You're barely old enough to boil water, but I suppose the company doesn't hurt. No one wants to spend time with someone considered old."

Again I didn't respond, just kept my eyes on her, waiting for something I could latch onto in such unfamiliar territory, perhaps a command or instruction.

"Can you read?" she suddenly asked, her sharp eyes turning to me as she took her time looking me over.

"Yes Ma'am." I responded quickly, "I'm the best reader at school."

She nodded her head. "Good, find a book on the shelf and read it to me."

I moved quickly in what would become a routine. I spent my afternoons after school reading to her. I became greedy for the words, desperate to finish the story so that I might be able to consume another one. Part of me worried that it would be taken away from me. Suddenly snatched from my hands. Mrs. Fields would provide me with this temporary bliss and then take it from me as quick as a switch. It was what I was used to, hope without actualization.

"Slow down," she would scold, angry that I was rushing the words someone had crafted so delicately and bravely. "You must read carefully otherwise you are wasting the words."

I found a pace, with time, which settled my burning curiosity and her need for a slow gentle build. The words had yet to be taken from me after months but still I waited. Knowing that this may be my one and only chance to grasp knowledge that wasn't otherwise available.

No matter how much I wished to stay and consume that little library until the sun burnt out, when the light hung low Mrs. Fields would send me away. Telling me that I should get home before it got dark.

"You never know what awaits you when there is the mask of darkness. Hurry along now. I fear a mother's wrath."

I would walk slower back home, letting the words settle with every step I took further away from my literary oasis. Trying to cling onto every word, engrave them into my soul so that I didn't forget a simple one.

On those walks home nothing would matter to me. The scenery around me would blur into itself and my mind would live in the pages I had consumed. Until I got to the road through the plantation. Every day without fail, Willy would be waiting there for me. His smile wide and his sweet brown eyes meeting mine as he welcomed me home.

A pink and purple sky fading to inky black behind him and making him more of a silhouette than a man. He would pull me tight to his chest, his body the strongest and warmest cage, protecting me from everything that threatened my routine. He would squeeze me so tight I couldn't breathe and then mutter into my hair.

"Welcome home, Stone." He had given me the name when I told him that rubies were actually just a type of rock. Nothing truly special about them. He had laughed and said I was the prettiest stone he had ever seen. His soft eyes always light with humor and love. I don't think Willy could ever hold any real malice for anyone. I had never seen anger or really even sadness in his eyes, just never ending joy.

We would walk side by side back to the house and he would ask me about what I had read. With vigor I would paint galaxies and worlds abroad for him. Trying to replace every word my eyes had soaked in with perfect accuracy, enjoying his laughs and smiles.

By the time we reached the small building we called home, the light had fallen and walking toward the orange glow of lantern light was the closest thing I could ever come to home. The light reached out for us, waiting until we were close enough to pull us in and wrap us tight.

The winter would be icy at this point, no light to heat us up and the sky cloud free so the heat ran away. We would be huddled close, the rough thread of our clothes doing little to keep the warmth in. We step inside and greet our parents, pulling ourselves to the table for a dinner of soup. Always soup.

If I allow myself the chance, my mind wanders to the potential. Who would I have been if I was born in Roswell instead of Black Town? Would my clothes be softer? My house warmer? Or is it not a matter of location but rather the darkness of my skin?

I would imagine a world where people walked beside me, happy to engage in light conversation. A place where belonging was normal and not something I had to search for. And I could read as many books as I pleased.

I couldn't let my mind wander on this topic for too long, I would make myself desperate and then angry.

But the road from this town to the next was a strange one, one that wound and bent in all directions. The people looked different on either end and they tasted their bread and wine with different hands. Black Town was drenched in need and want. A desperation that never ceased.

Chapter 2:

Cotton Fields Make For Unlikely Friendships

William Johnson was the best sort of person there ever was. He was sweet without it meaning anything and always minded his manners. It didn't matter who you were or how you treated him, you were worth respect in Willy's eyes.

His ability to see the good in people is something I both admired and frustrated me. I was far too volatile and quick to anger to always believe that people were good. I held grudges easily whereas he was quick to let them go.

He was made for the cotton fields, it was the place that he was happiest and most calm. He lived and breathed the fields and he knew more about cotton than most. Many of the sharecroppers worked on the plantations because it was the only thing they knew how to do or it was the only thing that they could do but my brother took to it like a fish to water.

Willy was my older brother by a good number of years but the only thing that would tell you that was his physique. He was a simple person and many people said that his mind often did not match up to his body.

I was often considered too inquisitive for my own good with a mind that could not be nurtured in the simple school of Black Town. My brother and I were in some ways complete opposites of each other.

"Mama, when will I work in the fields like Willy?" I had asked her when I was much younger.

She had looked surprised by the question but answered anyway "When you are needed in the fields."

"When will that be?"

"You might never work in the fields, Ruby," Mama had admitted.

I had hidden how relieved I was. The fields would never bring me fulfillment. I would be far too bored.

To me he had always just been Willy, my big, slightly clumsy, older brother. Mind you, he was never clumsy in his physicality but rather he was clumsy in his mind. He knew an awful lot about cotton and cotton picking but not much about anything else.

He had started in the fields younger than I was now and just a little before I had been born. Given the easy jobs like taking the baskets to the barn to empty them of cotton and then take them back to the fields.

Sometimes he would fetch water from the wells in large bucket's and carry them back to the fields during the drier months.

"He had these tiny, skinny little arms," Mrs. Mackenzie had told me one afternoon when Mama had sent me to fetch something from her. "I think that's why he grew to be so big, we all just kept feeding him because he looked like he was going to snap."

I had listened with wide eyes, to think at one point my brother had been smaller than me.

Willy quickly got more and more complex tasks on the plantations, being handed off the jobs they typically gave to the older children. He did them without complaint and a smile on his face.

"He's a hard worker that one," The other sharecroppers would murmur as they watched him in the fields, always the first to arrive, often the last to leave.

"Not much going on up inside his head though," They would laugh, shaking their heads.

Willy liked the cotton fields he often told me, I wondered if perhaps the cotton was his only friend. He would work on his own for the most part, sitting in tucked away spots as he diligently worked through the fields. Often talking softly to the plants and then telling silly jokes that the children made to the other workers.

The younger workers, the children liked him a lot. His soft nature when it came to speaking and how he was good for picking up the heavier and more difficult jobs. He would offer his help even if he had his own work to get through.

I was often reminded that my brother had lived a life before mine, and with time I started to take more notice of him. How he often knew more about the cotton than father, which was surprising because father knew *everything about* the plantations. But more often than not, father would have to ask Willy for advice and Willy always knew the answer and if he didn't he could figure it out. It was a shocking revelation, that there were things to learn in places that didn't interest me.

Cotton meant nothing to me and so it didn't really seem like there was anything worth learning when it came to it. It was just another thing in the world but that didn't mean that anyone had to think about it. I learnt quickly that I was very sorely mistaken about this, that sometimes people knew an awful lot more than you in areas you never wanted to know anything in.

He would listen carefully to me on our walks back from Mrs. Fields. When we would go back through the fields together, Willy would ask me all kinds of questions about what I had read, willing to listen. He often didn't understand much of it and I wasn't very good at explaining but he was always curious. A soft sort of twinkle in his eyes that surprised me.

But I could never tell if it was because it made me so happy to tell him or if he actually wanted to hear what I had to say.

There was a reason that everyone called him Big Willy. Willy was very tall and very broad, his muscles had been toned and bulked through the manual work on the plantations. He always seemed a little larger than life to me back then.

A bulging shadow of raw power and protection, something that could never be brought down. Many children look up to their parents but for me it was my brother. He was so much of what I sought to be in life. Kind, hardworking and never downed by anything. Never once had I seen him cripple under negative emotions. He was this positive force in my life.

People never seemed to get him right.

"Stay away from him, he's dangerous." Mothers would hush into their children's ears as they walked down the street, tugging them away and keeping them close. He did look dangerous, such a powerful body could only bring trouble.

"Not much going on in there, he's good for cotton picking and that's it," others would say, shaking their heads and sighing. He was only a cotton picker in their eyes. A boy who had never matured past the age of twelve. They didn't see the tender care in how he dealt with all people, didn't notice the sparkling interest in his eyes that burned to know more.

Even though I never got him quite right, I came close, at least I liked to believe that I did.

For the people that pushed through his tough exterior, he was a quick friend to most. He was easily amused and conversation was always light, a break from the grazing nature of the rest of the world.

He drew in all sorts but perhaps the strangest of all was Charlie Pickney.

Charlotte Raye Pickney was the most beautiful girl I had ever met. She was that classic sort of beautiful, shimmering blonde hair, bright blue eyes, and small dainty features to match. She was in the eye of many beholders and people often spoke of how easy it would be to marry her to a powerful family. Beauty like hers was often rare.

To me, she was beautiful not for her looks but for other reasons. First, it was her elegance, the grace that she carried herself with. It was the kind of posture that I associated with the princesses I had read about in books. An unyielding poise that often made you desperate to know more about her. She floated around the rooms. I had spent more time than I liked to admit mimicking the way she held herself with little success.

Mrs. Fields would tell me in my later years that her posture was not something you could really teach, you were either born with it or you were not. I liked to argue that money tends to play with your genetic pool a lot.

The second was the way in which she regarded people, it was a great similarity between her and Willy, she held people with kindness, no matter who they were. I never felt looked down upon or different when I was around her. She made me feel like an equal even though I knew that this simply was not the truth. Charlotte Pickney and I would never be equals. Yet she made me feel so.

She was a magnetic presence to be around. One I still have trouble describing. You never felt manipulated or out of your depth like other magnetic presences I have met in my life. You simply felt at home.

I first met Charlie on Saturday when Mrs. Fields had required my presence outside of the usual hours.

"Child," She had called to me as I was placing the choice book of that afternoon back on the shelf before I headed out for the evening.

"Yes ma'am," I had turned to her, folding my hands behind my back and standing straight like Mama had taught me to. However, I held eye contact like Mrs. Fields had taught me.

"I need your assistance this Sunday," She began, her face giving nothing of her thoughts away, " I am having some guests over and will need the extra hands to help wait on their needs and wants."

I nod my head, not fully understanding what she is saying to me but not really willing to ask for an explanation. She wasn't so forgiving to my questions.

"You will be *working*, not reading," She says sternly, "So I need you in your best dress and on your best behavior. Petunia will sort out the rest."

Petunia was the woman who had replaced my mother after she went to work for someone else. I had only spoken with her a few times but she was far too strung up to be so young and seemed to believe that she had some moral high ground over me.

She was rich in color but fair skinned in comparison to me. The kind of toning that would result in nasty words being yelled at her by the children of Black Town as she went about her day. Words I would never dare repeat in front of Mama.

"I have church on Sundays, Ma'am," I suddenly remember the stuffy tin roofed building I was forced to endure once a week, "What time would you need me?"

Her eyes are the same harsh gray but she looks at me with something I can only explain as surprise, like she isn't expecting me to respond with that. "They are only coming in the afternoon, head straight here after church and do not dawdle."

I nod my head quickly at her words and then excuse myself to head back home.

***

The Church of Black Town was the largest building in the town and had been built of brick with a tin roof that baked in the sun. There were windows all around the building, letting natural light in and ensuring that we didn't need too many candles in order to light up the room.

At the front of the room there was a podium where the pastor usually spoke and the rest of the room was filled with extremely uncomfortable pews and a small aisle down the middle. Behind the podium sat a large cross that was made up of various different pieces of wood all put together. It had been handcrafted by one of the men in Black Town.

I had never had much of an interest in church. The talking went on for a long time and the songs were boring and nothing like the pretty tunes Mama sang while she worked. I often ignored what was being said. The words were either very disheartening or seemed to me like a lot of promises.

Mama was often mad about my lack of interest in God but I couldn't find anything about the Church that wowed me. I would spend the morning staring out the window while I told stories to myself in my head.

Church had seemed longer than it ever had. The sermon droned on as I tried not to fidget or fiddle in my chair, lest I wanted to deal with the bruising command of my mother's hands. God was important to knowing which road to choose, how could you fiddle when god was speaking to you?

It had been a relatively hot day for the incoming winter, one that made me sticky and wanting to rip the thicker dress from my body, the one that had two skirts instead of one. The heat made the walk to Mrs. Fields nearly unbearable but I endured it for the sake of knowing what was awaiting me. Curiosity is a dangerous friend with no patience.

When I knocked on the door, it was not Mrs. Fields who opened it, rather it was a girl a couple of years older than me. I recognized her, she lived on the Pickney plantation and often stopped to talk to Willy on her way through the fields.

Willy seemed to like her a lot. They could talk about the books she was reading, ones that were filled with a lot more magic than the ones I devoured during the week in my secret oasis.

I had only seen them talking to each other a few times, a halo of secrecy encompassing every interaction. Something about their energy matched each other, a serene naivety to both of them that even I—so many years their junior—had lost.

But most of my experience of the girl was not through my own interactions but rather through Willy.

"Hello Big Willy," she would greet him as she headed to school in the morning, walking on the path through the fields, often near where he would work. She would be wheeling her bike beside her, the roads through the fields wouldn't always be designed for riding conditions.

"'Morning little Miss Charlie," he would respond with all bright smiles and soft eyes. He would ask her where she was heading so early and her response would be the same, "School of course."

I don't know how it started, how two strangers that saw each other in passing decided to break the quietness of their interactions in favor of potential. I often wondered why she spoke to him or started the friendship. What did she have to gain or to lose from it all? What I did know was that Willy went from never mentioning her at all, to speaking of her nearly every single day.

He would speak of her with a smile I had never seen before, the one you reserve for your first friend with the hope that you will keep it in place for eternity. It had been a bit of a shock for him to have someone in his life that I did not have in mine. Willy was friendly and kind to all but I doubted many people called him "friend."

He got along with all the other Black Town folks, was happy to help out when he could, and they often spoke of him kindly. Most found him too young for his body, his mind far too simple for the needs outside of cotton. He was sweet but not substantial and it made it difficult for others to interact with him. I only got along so well with him because there were so many years separating us. He stood on my level—neither above nor below me—rather at my side despite our ages.

I had been dismissive when he first brought her up, swallowed back some terrible words and changed the subject. Willy was my special person and I didn't want him to be taken by anyone else.

Perhaps it was a mere tolerance over repeated exposure, but I eventually learned to let his friendship with the Pickney girl be. I didn't like it but I also didn't want anything to stop the keen twinkle in his eyes, a shimmering connection that made him come alive.

It was only then, on that Sunday—sticky and hot—that I would meet the girl for myself for the first time.

She had opened the door and looked at me with mild recognition, like a face you aren't sure you have seen before or has the vagueness that some do. She smiles politely and then says, "How can I help you?"

I look at her for a long moment and then say "I work here." She looks a little bit taken aback, unsure if a single word that leaves my lips is the truth. She looks behind her, wondering if it is worth getting Mrs. Fields to come and see but eventually decides to step back and let me in.

I hurried back to the kitchen without bothering to answer any of her questions, I had strict instructions and I was not going to mess up on my first day of actual work.

The afternoon drew on. Mostly I spent it washing dishes and carefully placing things on plates. Petunia had said that I was still too untrained to take anything out into the sitting room and so I could help in the kitchen where I wouldn't be seen.

I was exhausted by the time I was allowed to go home, spending the entire day on my feet was not something I was used to and I wanted nothing more than for it to be time to sleep. Unfortunately, I still had a long walk home. And sure 'nough, the girl decided to accompany me on it.

I don't really know why Charlie chose to walk beside me, wheeling her pretty blue bike next to her. She could make the journey a lot faster had she ridden and left me to make my way back to my little house in the middle of the fields. But still, she chose my company as we walked through the fields in painful silence that I didn't even considered breaking.

My eyes took her in, watching her carefully through my periphery. The curve of her face is aristocratic. She was blissfully put together and I found myself in envy. There was a pretty blue bow in her hair, one made of the richest fabrics that doesn't fray and weather like the few that I had owned. I had wanted one of them desperately when I was younger, having seen it on a woman walking through the fields.

I study it. I wondered if she knew the worth of something so small. If she would cherish it like me.

"The color would look good on you." I started at the sound of her voice, broken from my wanting thoughts and being forced to make eye contact with her. She smiled at me sweetly and it is all teeth.

"I don't wear it very often. I prefer to keep my hair plainer but mother insisted that I wear it today. You have to look proper for certain events." she said. She is implying something with her words that I don't quite grasp. But I nod anyway, not willing to ask or learn.

She looks at me for a moment, studying my face and body. I don't know what she is looking to see but whatever it is, she finds it.

Quicker than I can blink, she pulls the bow from her hair to allow her golden tresses to drop, falling around her face. It makes her seem younger and older all at the same time. She pushes the bow into my hands, stopping for a moment to do so and then keeps walking.

I stare at it, unsure of why she gave it to me. It is so soft in my fingers, softer than cotton could ever be and I worry for a moment that I will ruin it by holding onto it. I trace it with a finger and holding it gently in my hand, taking hurried steps to catch up.

"You're Big Willy's sister right?" she asked me, not stopping or turning around. The soft bow was still tightly clutched in my fingers.

"Yer" I muttered. Had Mama heard me turning my words over so badly she would have had my head.

"Oh he's simply lovely," She said, her voice airy like a bird's song, "I would love to have him as my older brother. I'm sure you feel very safe around him."

I nodded noncommittally. If I was quiet enough and had enough patience, she would start to answer all the questions burning in my mind. People are willing to talk, if you give them a moment of silence. She didn't speak for a moment but the tension in her arms became unnatural and she awkwardly cleared her throat a number of times.

"He always greets me in the fields," she begins and now I am listening. Just who is Big Willy to Charlotte Pickney? "He's much easier to talk to than most people his age. He doesn't feel so overwhelming or intimidating. I really like talking to him."

I let her paint him with her words, turning the boy I know into something different from the familiar image in my brain. No two people will ever look at something the same and I drink in her explanation of my brother with an unyielding thirst. I need to know if others see him as I do. If my version of him, something I cherish deeply and possessively, is owned by anyone else.

She speaks of someone almost like a stranger but closer than my own skin.

A large, tall body that sticks out in the fields and on the horizon, he is the picture of strength and power. Intimidation rolling from every defined muscle and vein, a body that speaks of command, willing you to yield from one look. A man that should be avoided for what the temper beneath him brings.

"Mother says that the bigger the man, the greater the anger. And nothing is more dangerous than a man's rage." I want to disagree with her, she has clearly never experienced the fury of a mother. But still I remain quiet, nodding my head and letting her speak.

"I didn't realize that his name was Big Willy, but when he told me it made sense. His body is so large that it almost has to be acknowledged."

It is after these words that the hard painting of my brother begins to fade. In its place is something gentler. Something softer. She speaks of a man who can tell the easiest jokes, ones that do not need too much thought or consideration but get you laughing as easy as breathing.

Someone who is kind, offering to help in every way that is possible and willing to do so when asked. I begin to see this in my picture of him too. Something deeply kind and generous, never upset by being put out if it means lending a helping hand.

A softness to the large exterior that speaks of genuine interest in those that give him a moment of their life. Not many spare him time mind you. I want to tell her but I don't want to shatter her vision. So I keep quiet, but only in my voice. My mind soaks in every word she says.

"He's the kind of person, you know, you don't have to spend all this time trying to work him out. Trying to pick apart how he thinks or why he says certain things. He means what he says and says what he means." There is a certain joy to her voice, a recognition that only just starts to seep through.

I look at her for a long moment, wondering if she is starting to realize how there are no shades of black and white in the world, only muddy grays that are difficult to pick apart and change depending on the light behind them. I wonder, only for a moment, if her life has protected her in ways that mine never will. Only people like Willy are untouched by the contempt that sweeps across the people of Black Town, and even then, he is still rough around the edges.

As we turned into the plantation road, I saw him there with the sunset to his back, the light surrounding him in a way I had never seen before.

My brother looked larger than life for a moment and I understood why everyone calls him Big Willy, his body taking up the sunset so he is all I can see. I can feel the relief flooding my body as we walk closer. Not that I was uncomfortable with Charlie, but rather I knew down to the smallest parts of me that this person is safely wrapped into a human being.

I want to run to him, like a child does to their mother but I hold back. It's not that it wouldn't be appropriate, I am still a child in so many ways but I can't let myself do that.

He greets us with a smile, a little bit for me and a little bit for her. His hand comes up to ruffle my hair, a different greeting to hers.

"Good evening, little Miss Charlie, are you heading home?" he asks her.

"Yes, I am." She smiles back politely but not forcefully.

"I will walk you back then. It's getting late and these fields are filled with all sorts of things."

We begin to make the walk through the fields. The cotton is low enough that I can see over it but with the hanging shadows it feels vaguely like a forest, twisting and curling around us. Daring us to go deeper.

The conversation changes but I remain a mere observer, listening carefully to the lilt in their voices and accents. Less interested in the words and more in how they articulate them.

"Say it correctly," Mrs. Fields commands and I look back to the page. I know I didn't pronounce anything wrong. I'm not sure how else she wants me to say it but am determined not to ask for help.

"There is far more to words than their pronunciation. Intonation and tone tell you far richer truths than the words on their own do." I look at her for a long moment, trying to peel her want from under her skin without having to ask. Then I turn my eyes back to the page and start reading again. Trying to read the words the way they would have been written in my head.

Charlie and Big Willy spoke freely with each other, their words delivered with laughter. There is a lightness to both of them, one that you only get when you are around a person who makes you feel comfortable. Like all your words make sense and are taken as they are meant to be.

My steps fall shorter and I follow behind them, seeing them both differently and unable to decide whether or not I like the change.

We near the turn off for our house and I anticipate the next words directed at me.

"Stone, I will meet you back at the house. I need to make sure that Miss Charlie gets home safe."

"'Course. I'll tell Mama where you went," I say as I turn down the narrow less worn path through the fields, knowing that it leads to a small room with stiff blankets. A room that my exhausted body craves desperately.

I turn after a few steps to watch them disappear into the shadows. I feel my uneasiness flush from my body. I don't want to keep them from each other, I don't want to possessively keep Big Willy to myself when he had clearly found something uniquely his. So I let them go, watching as they match their steps and walk toward the sun. A friendship blooming like the cotton in the fields.

An unlikely friendship. One that has a defining point of when it dipped away from a stranger passing to a tightly knit jersey that wound warmly around two hearts.

How their friendship would ever be able to exist outside of those fields I did not know. Charlie could never tell her parent of her negro sharecropper friend, they would never allow it. Willy would never be able to bring his friend home to meet his parents. Mama wouldn't allow it.

You can't have a friend that is different to you. The whites see us as nothing but good workers or hardened criminals and we are constantly at the mercy of the white's rule. You cannot foster a friendship when one always has the power and the other is left groveling at your feet.

Still it seemed to work for them, in the fields where no one could see them. In the fields where they were people first and not defined by the richness of their skin and the amount of land they owned.

I look down at the bow still held in my hands and run my thumb over the top of it to smooth out any wrinkle from holding it so tightly.

Maybe she's not so bad.

Chapter 3:

Guilty Until Proven Innocent

Mrs. Fields had needed me there that weekend as she was having friends over. She didn't call them friends but I didn't like the wording she used. I felt that it was unlikely for Mrs. Fields to have any proper friends but I often hoped that maybe she would see me in a similar manner.

The women that flocked to her house on the odd Sunday were never the sort that I would spend my time thinking too deeply about. They wore beautiful dresses that spoke too loudly in the colors of their wealth and power. Bright pinks and purples that were more of an eyesore than they were fashion. They drank too much tea, the pot running empty, and when the tea was finished, they drank too much whiskey. They were loud with voices pitched too highly and syllables so airy it was hard to believe that they had anything of value to say.

I hated what they spoke about, all this talk about marriage and problems and runaway children and none of it seemed to matter.

I liked the gossip in Black Town, deep and meaningful. I knew the colors of the eyes that wept, I had touched the hands that harmed. It was personal and close to me, that kind of knowledge is important when it's all wrapped around your heart and soul, so close you can taste it. You can wield that sort of knowledge. But the baker's son who ran away with this-or-that plantation owner's daughter was not interesting nor was it valuable.

But I liked to listen, mostly because in the rare moment when the room went silent, Mrs. Fields would speak. All the women around her would lean closer, desperate to get a drop of her words to satisfy their thirst.

Mrs. Fields was the town gossip but in a manner that was dignified and profound. She knew everything about everyone but not the paper thin truths that people tried to use to veil who they really were, rather she knew the real nitty gritty details of the curling shadows that wrapped around people. She knew what people had done when their raw rage and greed bled so thickly that it became who they were. Petty stories meant nothing, but secrets, skeletons in closets were the most precious and dangerous of truths.

The only other saving grace, apart from those few moments that I heard about a humanity as messy and black as it was, was Charlie. If my presence was requested on a Sunday then I could be certain that Charlie would be there.

She was allowed to sit with the woman, sipping tea and eating the biscuits from the tin that I had to climb to reach. Those were the expensive biscuits, the ones saved for special occasions. I would learn in the years to come that Mrs. Fields made them herself. She would eventually show me the recipe and it would become a secret I held closer to my chest than any other. These biscuits were not the ones I chewed on after the long walk from school, but they were buttery and perfectly crunchy. I only knew this because Charlie snuck one or two into her dress for me whenever these events happened.

Charlie was often looked at with great envy. She was young and beautiful with a great family to her name. She held a certain power that many of the older women in the room only dreamed to taste. They regarded her with well-hidden distaste and spoke to her in backhanded compliments. Her nose would scrunch up all funny when they weren't looking and she would mouth things to me that I never understood but still made me giggle.

But I was still the help, so I had to hide my laughter behind well timed coughs and a quick scuttle to the kitchen to collect a new tea pot or some more snacks.

It had taken some time and command from Mrs. Fields before Petunia was allowed to be a server at these events and not just stuck in the back of the kitchen washing dishes and carefully pouring hot water into the pot for the next round of tea. I think she wanted me to listen in, wanted me to be there even if it was on the fringes. There was some lesson that she was intending for me to learn, although like all her lessons I was never sure exactly of what it was or how it would benefit. Her sharp eyes and high nose bridge were enough for me to not stomp my feet indignantly. She never told me what I was meant to get out of an experience, only asked me what I thought was valuable.

***

On my second Sunday of serving, I got to see the nastiness that was masked by the laughter and joyful behavior of the woman. I had been quietly standing in the corner of the room, waiting for someone to call me over if they needed something or for the call of Petunia when the fresh pot of tea was ready.

One of the women had, during a lapse in the conversation, snapped at me, "Can't you see that the biscuits are finished, go and get some more."

Surprise and a sudden command had made me snap to attention and hurry to retrieve the plate from the table and go to the kitchen. I rushed inside the kitchen and Petunia looked a little surprised to see me.

The woman who had commanded me was a thin lady with pinched features that made her look more animal than human. She held her nose up and it only made her more unattractive but these were things I realized after I met her.

"I need more biscuits please, Petunia."

She raised an eyebrow at me, looking me up and down before some sort of understanding pulled across her features and she nodded before turning to go and retrieve them from the cupboard.

"I am afraid we are out of biscuits," I stared at her, not understanding her properly.

"There are the ones in the blue tin," I say, knowing that we had not run out of the biscuits that I had during my reading session.

She simply shook her head, "We can't give them those ones, they are not good enough."

I swallowed thickly, body understanding that I was going to have to go back out and inform them of the situation. I pulled my hands behind my back after placing the plate and hurried back to the sitting room. Missing the remorseful way that Petunia was looking at me.

"There are no biscuits left Mrs. Fields," I addressed the lady of the house, keeping my eyes away from the woman that made me feel too small for the room.

"What did you say?" The woman snapped again before Mrs. Fields could respond.

"The biscuits are finished Miss" I said speaking politely and making eye contact.

Her face turned red and her nose scrunched unattractively.

"Then go get more!" She yelled, "Honestly how useless are you? If we want biscuits then you get them."

She shook her head and then said to the table like I wasn't in the room, "Honestly those Negros are good for nothing. They can't even teach their children to fetch. What a waste of space."

The other woman in the room laughed loudly at her words, expressing her agreement and I pulled back, standing as close to the wall as I could hoping that they would forget that I existed.

"I don't think we need more biscuits Agatha, the afternoon is nearly over," Mrs. Fields had cut through the laughter and as quick as lightning they had all pulled into themselves like nothing had happened in the first place.

"What does the word Negro mean, Mrs. Fields?" I had asked when all the women had left and gone home. She sighed, for the first time looking old and tired.

"It's a word for Black people, Ruby. It is meant to shame and undermine you. Make you less." She didn't look at me as she said it, still reading her book and then looking out the window.

"Oh," I said. It had never felt good when someone had called me that but it had more to do with how they said it and less about the word itself. It was starting to take on its own new personality.

I never saw that woman over for tea after that, it was my first and only experience with her. Mrs. Fields probably didn't invite her back because she didn't like that sort of company. When all the women had been laughing, she had a frown on her face.

***

Standing in the corner of the room with my back to the wall, quietly listening in even without ever having a say or being allowed to act like I was even there was far better than scrubbing dishes. Petunia had the tendency to breath down my neck and make me rewash things if she didn't think I had done a good enough job.

Today's tea had started later than normal, the sun already starting to dip heavily into the sky and make everything seem yellow-swept. I had spent the morning cleaning around the room under the stern guide of Petunia and listening to Charlie receive a lesson in etiquette. It was the reason that she saw Mrs. Fields on the weekends but they really ever did a proper lesson. Unless Mrs. Fields had something in particular she wanted to go over.

"Why did you do that with Charlie?" I had asked her one Monday after having witnessed the girl balancing books on her head while pretending to eat.

"Charlotte." Mrs. Fields corrected.

"What?"

"Charlotte, you are to refer to her as Charlotte to those older than you and when someone says something that you don't understand you say 'pardon' not 'what'."

I stared out the window for a moment, pondering her words.

"Why do I have to call her Charlotte if she lets me call her Charlie?" I finally ask, fiddling with the skin around my nails and not able to make eye contact with Mrs. Fields. Every part of me restrains against the idea.

"There are some social rules that don't make sense, Child, but still we must follow them. Not out of respect or class but out of self-preservation." I looked up at her after she spoke. This lesson was written across her face as clear as day. I didn't need her to completely understand what she was trying to tell me. Even then, my throat burned with bile and a sense of morality I wished I never had.

"And to answer your previous question, I am teaching her etiquette," The older woman said before gesturing for me to pick up the book and continue reading. I would ask her what the word meant, as I had never heard it before but decided I would look it up in the dictionary on the table before I had to go home that day.

When the woman had started to arrive at an unknown time, I had found myself pulling toward my body. I never hunched over or made myself small, mostly because Mrs. Fields would not stand for it but there are many other ways to go unnoticed. To remove your presence from a room without physically leaving.

I brought tea to the table, refilled cups and ensured that the plates never ran empty all without so much as a glance my way, returning to my corner where I waited and listened carefully.

Something in the air was different today, there was a buzz amongst the women, one of them in particular, but something had happened. I could taste it, sweet and foreboding on my tongue.

They were patient with it, didn't blurt it out like normal, all of them glancing at each other and trying to decide when was the best time to let the story be presented. There were nudges and careful suggestions that caught my interest. Making me listen to everything a little more closely, holding onto the breaths between the words.

Finally, during a moment of settled emotions, one of the women leaned back and she commanded the room. I didn't know her name, but I knew she was the most lavishly dressed, her wealth and status falling from her clothes in a way that was almost comical. A desperation to seem wealthier that it only made her look like a cheapened version of those occupying the room with her. She had a smile on her lips, one that screamed "I know something that you don't."

"There was quite the disturbance at the market this morning," She begins, picking her cup and saucer up to swirl the spoon around. Her voice sounds strange, disinterested. Usually she would be dripping with emotion but right now she sounds like she is sharing how her roses have been doing.

"Was there?" Mrs. Fields began, "I'm afraid I missed it, please do enlighten me."

I lean forward, watching the twitches in body language, the tug of lips. Whatever this is, I will not miss a second of it.

"Some poor little boy got accused of stealing," She says, her lips twisting and curling.

"Came all the way from Black Town, tiny little thing never should have made the trip on his own but you know how negligible they are down that way, to get some things -"

"Can't imagine they have much variety," Another woman interrupts her and misses the sharpening of the speaker's eyes.

"-from the general store" She finishes, her eyes once again being drawn back to Mrs. Fields. "Bought everything no problem, paid and left. But when he started walking back, the shopkeeper ran out claiming that this young boy had stolen."

My eyes furrow as I listen, why would he steal? Black Town folk only ever came to Roswell for the rare things that we couldn't make or get ourselves and we kept our trips short. People stared for too long, nasty spit-filled words thrown our way. Stealing wasn't just drawing attention to yourself but it was damning the entire town. There had to be more to it.

"Well did he?" Mrs. Fields prompts.

"Little sugar claimed that he didn't, promised that he hadn't taken anything other than what he had paid for." He spoon clinks against the side of her cup, ringing out in the room clear and harsh. There is a heavy tone of unbelieving in her voice, a certainty in the idea that the child had been lying.

"He even turned out his pockets and his bag to show that he hadn't taken anything but the shop keeper was positive of what he knew. There was something missing and the boy had to have taken it."

"Poor thing was quite shaken, the man was getting very threatening and there was no way he could prove it when all he had was his word." She lets the words hang heavy in the air, brushing against everyone's ears and swirling thickly inside our heads. So much behind them, I don't like how she says them, something in her tone makes me feel angry. My skin was hot and flushed.

"The man was in a rage I heard, screaming all kinds of things at the boy," She lifted her hand to tuck a strand of hair behind her ear before she imitated the man, "'This little nigger-child stole from me. I know he did! Good for nothing. Goddamn niggers, always causing trouble! Especially in my shop!' You would never believe that a Negro child could go white but this one did."

"And?" Mrs. Fields again. Her voice is clear and unencumbered with emotional pursuit.

"Well, the Pastor came to his rescue," she says after a pause far too long, "Says that he saw those bad seeds taking things and had just gone to tell him when he heard the commotion outside. He assured the shop keeper that the boy had done nothing wrong and sent him on his way."

She waves her hand, unhappy with the anticlimactic end to a story. The damnation of these bad seeds is far less interesting than that of a wandering boy of different complexion.

"Honestly, I think it was good of the store owner, that negro child will start stealing one day, best to catch him early." I held back my anger and listened to the other words.

"True," another woman adds, "Negros ALWAYS grow up to cause problems in society. No manners, such lowly beings."

The others all nodded their heads and looked as if they felt pity for us. Not that they could feel anything for us when they misunderstood us so deeply.

My chest feels tight as an iron taste fills my mouth, the effort of not taking this woman down kicking bleeds heavy in my mouth. Her words are even what makes me so bridled with rage, rather it is the way that she says them.

"A pity that such a thing could happen." Mrs. Fields says, drawing her cup to her mouth. I am not sure if she is referring to the event or the women's attitudes. The room seems to suddenly sag and collapse in on itself, the anticipation drawing to a pinnacle and then dropping, uneventfully into nothing. None of the women had been expecting such a simple response to the event they had been building up all morning. The speaker particularly seems disappointed, she had been hoping for something else, a different sort of reaction.

"Shall we have some more biscuits?" Mrs. Fields diverts and I am back to making rounds.

***

I have just taken the last of the china to the kitchen when I hear Mrs. Fields address Charlie for the first time since all the women filtered out of the house.

"If you keep pulling a face like that, you might be stuck with that expression for the rest of your life Charlotte." I step back into the room and am suddenly aware of the pulsating heat coming from the older girl. Her cheeks are flushed with her rage and her eyes are dark, eyebrows drawn close.

She clenches her jaw a few times before she opens her mouth to speak, "How could they do that?"

"Whatever do you mean Child?"

"How could that shop keeper just treat that poor boy like he is nothing but a thief when they had no proof? Something missing and he automatically assumes it's just some innocent boy? How can you do that?" Charlie looks up and her eyes are watery. I never thought anger could be anything but fire, but this water, this tumultuous ocean in her eyes feels far more dangerous.

"That man, acted on his conditioning child. He did not think or look to reason to solve his problems," I don't fully understand the response but still I watch on, deeply wrapped in my curiosity.

"But it's not *fair*." Charlie blurts out, crossing her arms as she sulks in her righteousness and necessity for change.

"The world isn't fair child," Mrs. Fields throws the words out like she is saying good morning, taking a sip of her whiskey before turning her sharp eyes on Charlie.

"There are some places that were never meant for people, they are bitter and hateful. These places are like salty soil, there aren't many plants that can grow in salty soil and the ones that do are horrid weeds that are as salty and bitter as the soil they grow in. People are fearful of what they do not know or understand, if something looks different to them then it simply must be different. This makes them afraid, different is dangerous and fear makes people hateful."

She pauses for a moment and then her eyes turn to me, her gaze calculated, "No matter our skin, we are all still people. Identical and completely opposite in all aspects. Skin does not define a person, actions do."

I feel my throat go dry as I struggle to swallow and breathe in her words. I don't say anything or add to the conversation, something about the intensity of her gray eyes, so stormy and forthcoming makes all thoughts in my head stop. Except for one, I am not my actions. Not in the way that Charlie is. I am all the precursors to my actions, all the heavy laid beliefs that outline my being. This lesson I learn without having to be told. Perhaps it was the most important one I would ever learn. But learning through words and through experience are two very different things.

The light coming through the window catches Mrs. Fields' eye and she sits up, breaking the moment apart and opening. "Well would you look at that, you two best be getting back or you will be walking in the dark."

Neither of us move for a moment. Charlie and I stare at each other, a conversation of understanding and grief pulling taunt between us before we are ushered again to leave.

"Hurry now, don't dawdle." Mrs. Fields says, standing up to guide us to the door.

We are out and walking down the street in no time, the bicycle our only companion. That and the setting sun, sitting heavy and red on the horizon. An indication of the winter slipping away from us as we stumble and fumble toward summer.

I wanted to ask her so many things on that walk back, a thousand little questions about why and when. Why did she care so much for that little boy? When did she start saying us as people?

I yearned to dip inside the walls of her skull and peel back her mind so that I could understand her a little better, know how she thought and why she thought like that. She had no necessity or need to pain and bruise over the injustice of the world, she was safe and sheltered from it but still she did.

But I just couldn't get the words out.

As we walked down the road together, I felt the words and ideas burn hot and heavy inside of me like a churning and bubbling soup that has been left unstirred. I tried to mix it all up to get a coherent sentence out, to find the words that would correctly articulate just what I wanted to say but they stayed as ever popping bubbles. Never living long enough to become coherent.

I opened and closed my mouth over and over again, trying to aid the sound in being pushed out but still we walked in silence. The sun burned redder and colder as it descended, my arms pulled tight to my body to keep me warm and still we walked in silence.

I watched as the wide fields too far to reach drew in tight next to us, so close that I could pick the cotton off the plants and then we turned down our road.

Big Willy wasn't waiting where he usually was but he had taken to waiting further down by the road to our house on these weekend evenings, meeting us where we split off so that he could walk Charlie home. I was used to it just being us for the last little stretch before I watched him walk her away as I hurried home to help Mama with dinner.

I was still struggling for my words, desperate to try and find something and anything to say. So she knew I understood to some extent that she saw me for what I was and not what I was ought to be. My eyes were not focused on the path ahead but rather the elongated shadows running under the plants, so I hadn't realized that Big Willy and Charlie were already walking away.

"Th-" I start but then quickly look around to spot the head of blonde hair. They are already some way ahead of me. Making a quick decision, I quickly followed along behind them, sticking to the fields so they wouldn't see me if they were to turn around. Unless they knew where to look.

I walked softly, pushing back the overarching branches of the cotton plants and hurrying alone until I was far enough that they couldn't hear me but I could hear them.

They were walking silently next to each other. Usually they made light conversation with each other but the atmosphere was heavy with the weight of the setting sun. I couldn't see their faces but I could only imagine the heavy frown turning Charlie's features and the perplexed tug of Big Willy's eyebrows.

"Big Willy?" Charlie asked him suddenly, the light of the farm house just starting to glint onto the path, reaching out to everything around them.

"Yes, little miss?" He responded, his entire body turning to give her his attention.

"I wish people could just live, without all the stuff in between." She says it so softly that I almost miss it. Big Willy keeps looking at her, watching her face as they walk and after a moment that feels too prolonged and silent he speaks.

"Me too little Miss"

They take a couple of more steps before he speaks again.

"That's what I like about the fields so much, all of us are the same in the fields."

"Sorry?" she questions, turning to look at him.

"In the fields, all of us are working to earn our keep, it doesn't matter if you own the farm or simply work there, you all have the same goal. All of us are the same out here. We all hold the same amount, we are all just people."

They keep walking without anything else being said until the point where Charlie turns to say goodbye and then rides off on her bicycle. Big Willy watches her go before turning around and heading home, whistling a pretty tune as he does so.

I watched him for a bit, not moving from my space crouched between the plants, not wanting him to know that I had intruded on this moment that was only meant for two. I watch him get far enough and then I cross to the other side of the field and hurry through the plants to make it back before him.

I wish my mind was as simple as his, wish it saw the world in beautiful colors and not muddy browns and grays. Big Willy truly believes that here in these fields we are all equal, as if nothing would ever separate and segregate us from each other. That in the fields we are nothing more than people working toward the same goal.

If that were true, I would sleep on a bed filled with warm sheets like Charlie, not on the floor of a tin home that was too cold in winter and too hot in summer. If that were true he would have gone to school and I would be allowed to study for as long as I wanted. I would not be bound to a job simply because of my circumstances and appearance.

The fields might make things more even, people might work side by side with each other but at the end of the day there are still the ones who owe and the ones that own.

Chapter 4:

Rotten Seeds Still Grow

As spring burned quickly onto the oncoming summer, the biggest change was always the dust. It seemed to stir up into the air with drying heat and coat everything it touched. It got into your eyes making it difficult to see.

I think I remember that day even more because of the dust that was clinging to everything. The first dusty day of the season.

It had been a Saturday, I had no obligations in Roswell and so I had been allowed out to play with the other children.

We were playing games in the dirt, drawing up complex chess boards and sports fields for us to play. The stakes were high and we fought tooth and nail against our enemies. Pushing and shoving to win, not caring for our dirtying clothes and bruising bodies. These were bruises that came from joy and laughter and nothing bad could be caused by those types of bruises.

We had tired as the day had grown hotter, the sun beating heavily down on our ebony skin and making us sticky and uncomfortable. Retreating to the shade of the trees at the edge of the town while we sipped on too watered down juice one of the children's parents had brought for us.

I was chatting with one of the children whose name I can't remember now when my eye caught sight of something happening a little way from us.

Three people, one of the little boys whose parents worked on the Pickney Plantation with mine and two older and taller white boys. I recognized them too.

Edward Rutledge and Thomas Drayton, two peas in a pod. We knew them more as Eddie and Tubby but the only thing that was sweet about them was their name.

They were standing over the little boy, I think his name was Toby, a tiny little thing with not much meat on his bones. He was very polite and all the other children were fond of him. Even from here, I could sense how intimidated he must have felt by them. Their bodies leering over him.

One of the white boys, Tubby I think, shoved his shoulder and Toby stumbled a few steps back. Eddie and Tubby laughed at him and then Eddie began to say something to Tobias. I doubt it was anything good just but the way Eddie's face contorted full of hideous emotions that had no place here. That and how Toby began to tremble and curl into himself. I stepped forward. I wanted to see a little more and get a better idea of what was going on.

Tubby shoved him again and this time he fell, fumbling to the ground. It didn't look too painful but still I didn't like watching it, my face pulling tight as I stared. He got up quickly Toby, I had to give him credit for his bravery even in this situation.

Him standing up had stopped the two whites' laughter and replaced it with anger. They were not happy that he was trying to stand up against them. Trying to some degree to fight back.

Tubby shoved him again, again he fell but this time, before Tobias could get back up, Tubby's fist connected hard with the boy's cheek. There was a loud smack that I could hear from where I was standing and my rage boiled. I was going to stop this and get these awful creatures hands off of one of my own.

I stepped forward, fully ready to march over there and give these children a piece of my mind when a hand grabbed my arm and stopped me.

"Don't." One of the boys I had been playing with stopped me. He was older than me and nearly the same size as Eddie and Tubby and he looked at me with an indifferent hardness that confused me.

"Why? We can help him." I exclaimed, gesturing to the boy who was being pushed down and into the dirt now.

"No we can't." He shook his head.

"But-"

"We will only make it worse, they will only blame us," He spoke with conviction and was already pulling me away from the scene. I began to fight back, trying to pull my arm free from his hold and get over there to help the boy who had blood running down the side of his face. He was choking on mouthfuls of sand while everyone either watched or pretended that they couldn't see.

"He's hurting!" I exclaimed.

"And they're white!" He yelled back at me, turning around to meet my eyes. Finally I could see the anger at the injustice in them.

"That doesn't matter, wrong is wrong." I asserted, so sure of myself, so confident in the rules of the world.

"Of course it matters! It always matters!" He grabbed me by the shoulders and spoke to me with a conviction that nearly scared me, "We will never, *never* be equals with them. Whites words will *always* matter more than ours and if we step in, those boys will only find a way to punish us and it will reflect on our parents."

"We can lick our wounds," he adds with a breathless voice. "We can pick him up and make sure he is alright *after* they have left, but only after. Trying to fight back will only make it worse."

"Because we're powerless?" I asked. No one had ever spoken about the strained rope between the Whites and Blacks in this area so bluntly before.

"Because we are Black. Because Black means *nothing* but problems here."

I ripped away from him and stormed away.

I felt sick, vomit building up in the back of my throat. How could they let something so clearly wrong just go untouched. Go unregulated. There were ten of us there, we easily could have chased them off. And yet…

And yet I was suddenly so unsure of myself. Right and wrong had always been clear to me but now, now it was blurring. Why did being Black meant that we had to take getting hit with a bit of tongue.

I got far enough away and then I was retching over to the side of the road, my juice and breakfast all coming up. For the first time in my life I burned with hatred for the two boys who use every inch of power that they have to do whatever they want. If I could I would burn them.

My rage and anger over all my encounters with them would be met with the same response.

"It's just the way it is."

I would be told over and over again. As a child you have a sense of justice, right and wrong seems to be set in stone. But everything that is wrong becomes right if you have the money for it. The people of Black Town, we had none.

Even then, I quickly learnt that not giving them a reaction meant they got bored and tried to find a more dramatic child to entertain them.

***

"You know something about bad seeds, Stone," Big Willy told me one day, sitting in the setting sun as we played a game in the sand, "Everyone thinks they're bad because they don't grow but that's not the case, they often grow better than the good seeds."

"Then what makes them bad?" I had asked, for the first time, to be interested in cotton.

"The fruit, the produce is what's often bad. They never produce anything worthwhile, only take up too much space and grow too quickly. But you ne'er get any good cotton off them." He had turned to be, his eyes still with the glinting innocence I knew so well yet so much younger.

"That's why we have to check the seeds so carefully." He smiled, and I nodded. Checking the seeds had been Mama's job. I would often help but never understood why it was so important. Seeds were seeds. The ground they were planted in mattered more, did it not?

The first time I had met Eddie and Tubby, I had been walking home from school. I was walking along the main path through the fields and didn't hear them coming up behind me.

"Aren't you supposed to be working," the slightly taller one snapped at me, then I hadn't know their names.

I turned around to make sure that it wasn't me that they were addressing only to be surprised to realize that it was me that they were speaking to.

"Are you dumb?" he asked me. Sadistic amusement on his face.

"No sir, I don't work in the fields, I'm heading home." I responded by trying to be polite and then turning to be on my way.

"I wasn't done talking to do," He snaps and I turn back around waiting for him to start speaking again.

He does say anything, just staring at me with red ears. The other one, the shorter one stands off to the side, his posture indicating that he is waiting for something.

A hand comes to settle on my shoulder and the taller boy leans back.

"Hattie Mae is asking for you back at the house Ruby," a rumbling voice speaks and I recognize it as one of my father's friends from the plantation. He is a friendly man and nearly as big. I nod my head and quickly hurry back home. Feeling dark angry eyes on me for a long time.

There are rotten seeds in every society, the sorts of people that even if you bring them up with the strongest hand and the most discipline they still turn out as the burnt ends of society.

I used to be enraged by their attitude and decisions. They had so much more that I would ever be allowed and yet they skipped school to play bad jokes on everyone. I couldn't stand that they were wasting something I desperately clung to. Perhaps they don't understand the value of something when it has always been a given.

***

"We need your advice Baba."

My father was not the oldest of the men in Black Town but he seemed to be the most respected. He had been the first to jump on the opportunity of being a sharecropper and held a good steady relationship with Archibald Pickney Jr. The owner of the plantation we lived on.

The residents of Black Town and the plantations often looked to my father for advice on issues arising on the plantations, he was a good friend and an even better leader. I had grown accustomed to regularly having visitors after supper who would come to speak to my father. Listening through the crack in my door was one of my favorite ways to get information about what was happening.

I let my parents usher me into my room when this particular guest arrived, used to having to hide when the necessary adult conversations took place. With practiced ease, I left a small crack open in my door, enough to allow the sound into my room and for me to watch everything that went on outside the door.

Sitting carefully, I pressed my back to the wall and listened.

"What is it? Something with the owner?" My father asked as my mother poured strong tea into enamel cups and sat quietly to the side, listening in but not involving herself in the conversation.

"No, no, it's not the owner," I couldn't see what the man did after that but he seemed to shift in his chair like he was uncomfortable.

"It's the Drayton and Rutledge boys." The man spoke with caution, like he was worried there were ears listening in to what he was saying. I knew he was talking about everyone in Black Town and Roswell did. Eddie and Tubby were practically sewed together at the hip. But they were dark children, they caused too many problems for both towns. They were well known as the bad seeds around these parts.

"What about them?" My father asked, leaning back in his chair so I could now see the man's face properly in the light of the oil lamp.

He was a young fellow, but his face was weather by the sun and fields. He looked too young and too old all at the same time. Maybe in a different world he would be able to be young for just a little while longer. The fields were no place for a child.

"Well they 'ave been causing some problems in the fields," his face pinched tight with the memory.

"Like what?" My father said, a gentle firmness that was unusual to me. I would never consider my father to be a gentle man but in this moment he seemed that way. His blood pumping with the woes and concerns of others.

The man opened his mouth once, twice, and then spoke, "They like to run through the fields, they trample some of the crops and tip over the picking baskets."

"I see." My father waited, knowing there would be more if he was patient. People talk when you give them silence.

"And when we aren't around the houses, they go there to mess with the children. They hurt my little John. He came home covered in bruises, took us a fair minute to get him to tell us what happened." The man's eyes seemed to shine a little more intensely, he took a shuddering breath before continuing.

"They don't like our kind, use every opportunity they have to show that. Making our work long and hard with all the games they play in the fields. "

"Have you tried to get them to stop?" My father asked. Which made sense, they were adults and these were nothing but boys pretending to be men, the sharecroppers to some extent owned the land and were allowed to tell the boys off if they got in the way of their work.

"We 'ave. But those boys, they don't see us as nothing but cotton pickers. We aren't people to 'em. We just don't know what to do." The man looked up now, staring at my father with a hope like I had never seen before.

"I see how that is a big problem, I can't say I have ever dealt with something similar." He rubbed his chin as he conceded that fact, taking the time to think about the situation before he spoke.

"You will need to speak to Mr. Drayton and Mr. Rutledge about it." My father looked at the man. The man's face twisted with worry and panic as he began to shake his head at my father's words.

"Well can't you see, it's their kids. Those folk, they don't take well to words about their children."

A very fair point. Even I, a mere child, knew now badly the plantation owners took to the sharecroppers speaking on their families and children. We were still their workers and served them, no matter how pretty the law seemed.

Studying the man before him, my father thought for a moment longer. The flame flickered and their shadows danced on the walls. I found myself leaning closer to hear better.

"Raise a general issue then," my father suggested. "Mention that it is children doing it but maybe don't specify who. You have to speak to them, if you don't then you will bear the consequences of staying quiet later."

He looked at my father as he ponded his words, before he began to nod. Agreeing with what had been said.

"Thank you, I will speak to the others and get in touch with the owners."

The room fell silent, the world drawing a little darker and heavier but still holding onto its light.

"Those boys have always been bad seeds, rotten to the core the day they were born." Mama said, shaking her head as she looked to the side. Even from my odd position and in the yellowing light, I knew the hardening look in her eye.

It was the same one she gave me when I stepped out of line. "That is not how Johnson's behave, Child!" I could hear her voice ringing clear and loud in my ears.

"Right you are Miss Hattie Mae, I never understood how a child could turn out like that. The man sighed and took a sip of his tea for the first time since arriving. If he found it bitter it didn't show on his face. I felt myself shivering at the mere thought of my mother's brew.

"I think in this case it is of no cause of their parents, they were simply born that way." Mama said with a pitying tone like that. Some people were just born bad. I would come to learn. The only thing they knew in life was how to hurt others.

"Still, a childlike that would never be allowed to run around in our parts. Even if the parents didn't set them straight, I certainly would." The man responded, shaking his head as he did. He didn't take another sip of the tea.

My father leaned forward, obscuring my view. "We are of different cotton threads."

There was a finality to that statement and I was leaning away and pressing my back into the wall. The conversation turned to children and the prices at the general store, nothing that interested me.

As my parents walked him out of the house and I crawled to my mat to pretend that I had been asleep the whole time, I found a thought coming to me. It was a terrible thought, one I often regretted thinking. One that would return to me in many moments after.

I thought of how different I would have been had I been born as Charlie Pickney and not Ruby Johnson. I thought of all the things I would never have to think of if I had been born into a house where I slept on a bed and not a mat.

***

I knew Eddie and Tubby were bad seeds, as sure as anyone else. But I had for the most part been removed from the rot that stretched out around them. They were not fond of my quick tongue and only ever encountered me in the fields where there were often too many witnesses.

There, with cotton blooming around me, I was in my element, one that they were unfamiliar with and didn't dare to touch.

But then I started working for Mrs. Fields and suddenly I was out of my domain and into theirs.

Still, the first couple of months I never really interacted with them, I had seen them picking on some other kids in the town but usually they were shooed away by store owners or parents before I could step in. Mama would kill me if I did. They were older and bigger than me and that only meant trouble.

"Your smart mouth will get you into trouble one day, Ruby," she had said as she slammed a blunt knife into potatoes, preparing the vegetables for that night's soup. "Nobody likes it when someone is smarter than them, especially if it's a child."

I hadn't responded, just nodded like I was meant to but I knew that I disagreed with her. If people didn't like others being smarter than them then they should simply read more. No one was smarter than Mrs. Fields and she was very respected.

When I wasn't walking to and from my after school activity, I was inside Mrs. Fields house, a place those two troublesome boys could not enter so I remained for a good while, safe from their games and malicious intentions.

But it happened every so often that Mrs. Fields needed me to run out and get her a few things. She was not fond of going out when she didn't need to, especially now that the sun baked and cracked the concrete with its intensity and I didn't really mind doing the quick run. It did cut down on my reading time, but it also meant that I got nice biscuits for tea.

The other few times I had done this I had been safe from any interruptions but this time, I was not so lucky.

Mrs. Fields often gave the exact amount that I needed but today, due to low stock, I had extra change from the trip that I had placed carefully in my pocket while I carried the items in a paper bag in my arms. But the coins played a pretty tune in my pocket with every step, unknowingly making me a target.

I didn't think much of the noise, it was an interesting addition to my walk and I found myself bouncing and changing my regular gait to control and play around with the sounds. I was nearly back, just a house or two down from Mrs. Fields when I was stopped rather abruptly by two bodies.

Looking up, I recognized the two boys almost immediately. The one was taller, a long and lithe body with pinched boney features. He was not dissimilar to a rat I had often thought but did well to keep that thought to myself. He was always accompanied by a sneer across his face, making him seem even more rodent-like. But best of all was his voice, it was pitchy and high as it had yet to drop like a mans. No matter how big he tried to make himself seem, he shrunk down smaller with a very badly disguised crack in his voice.

They had grown up together on the plantations, being close friends since birth but they had been allowed to run free their entire lives without much consequence and that was the first problem.

Together they wound tighter and tighter until they moved like one person, their bodies and desires woven together and drawing them into one person. And it was in the tight knit embrace that the rot began to grow.

"Where ya heading to?" He asked me, puffing his chest out and looking down at me over his sharp nose. Edward Rutledge had a lot of bark.

My eyes turned to the one standing next to him, he was shorter and rounder. But his plush body was never to be mistaken for weakness. He held an unsuspecting strength. Thomas Drayton's soft baby face made him seem sweet, delicate and I am sure he would have been if he hadn't been so caught up with Eddie. Or maybe he too was simply a bad seed.

"Mrs. Fields." I said simply, not bothering to look at him. He simply wasn't worth my time and not engaging them was far better than any other strategy.

"If you could let me through, she wanted me to run the errand for her in a cotton picking minute," I tried to step forward, hoping that they would move apart so I could get back. They didn't budge and I found myself taking an even larger step back to try and create distance between.

Annoyance, bubbling and hot sung under my skin, if they could simply get out of my way then none of this would be a problem. The money wasn't mine, it was Mrs. Fields and so they would be stealing from her and not me, that was far worse of a crime, but clearly their lack of interest in school had made them slow.

"We just need to relieve you of your change, tax for walking down this road," Eddie had smiled as if he thought himself to be clever. He clearly didn't know what the word meant. Probably heard his Daddy say it and used a word other children didn't know to get what he wanted, but I did know what it meant.

"Do you own this road?" I asked him. Now looking in his eyes as I did so.

He laughed but it was unsure and angry, "I don't need to."

"You do," I stated, clearly he didn't understand how tax worked, "If you want to take tax."

He stared me down, something unreadable on his face. Her features scrunched together, a weak sort of anger pulling them together and transforming his confusion to rage.

"Tubby, take it." He commanded and with practiced ease, Tubby moved toward, not even letting a sound past his lips as he reached for me. I was pulling away, fear suddenly wrapping around me when I had been so confident and then-

"Ruby, what on earth is taking you so long?" Mrs. Fields was standing in all her beautiful authority, her dress making her drip of money and her hands on her hips as she stood a few feet away studying the situation carefully.

I had been startled by my name, not used to hearing her call me anything other than "Child". Still relief fills me when seeing her. "Did I not tell you that I needed you to be quick?" She added at the end, raising her eyebrow at me.

"Yes, Mrs. Fields." I responded dutifully, trying to stop myself from smiling.

"Then why are you just standing there?" She asked me. I knew she knew what was going on but she wanted me to say. Words are far more condemning than a moment taken out of context.

"They won't let me through." I gestured to the two boys, they hadn't said anything but were looking back and forth between us.

Her eyes narrowed, "Right," She drawled out, "Boys do you not have something better to be doing this afternoon?"

Both of them hesitated, looked at each other for some kind of explanation of what they should do. Eventually it was Tubby who spoke, much to my surprise, "No, ma'am"

"Well find somewhere else to play games, people live here and have business to attend to." She dismissed them with a wave of her hand and beckoned me to come. This time when I stepped toward them, they parted quickly and let me through. Mrs. Fields began to lead me back to the house, a hand on my shoulder before she stopped and turned to the boys once more. They were only just beginning to leave.

"And boys," She said, her voice verging on threatening. "If I ever hear about you terrorizing my employees again then I will need to give your parents a call. Children must grow up at some point."

The last bit she added on much softer, I don't think they heard but still they paled at her words. Their eyes darted around and they were dashing off quickly after all of that.

I found it interesting that their parents seemed to evoke such fear within them. Clearly they were not high and almighty about everything in their life, there were things that could scare them.

Perhaps my father had been right when he had spoken to that other sharecropper about talking to the boy's parents. There was still some sort of hold on them, but whatever it was it didn't stop them from their actions. They still played unkind tricks and picked on the children. However one thing was certain, they only did it when they were certain the information wouldn't get back to their parents.

It made even more sense now, why they favored the Black Town children, we had no way of speaking up. They were free to do as they pleased in our town and their fields.

To the children of Black Town, Eddie and Tubby were a swear. They were vengeful spirits that came in and ruined all of our games. None of the children could stand the thought of them and every single one of us had at least one story of them terrorizing us.

They were worse than just bad seeds, they were rotten and rot had a tendency to spread.

Chapter 5:

What Did He See?

"I saw it."

It's near damning the weight of a white folk's words. No matter whether it is a child or an adult. The white children have more power than a Black man. Their value weighs more on the scales we call society. They are simply more honest.

"I saw him."

How can anyone really understand a moment? Sometimes you look at something thinking it to be a person and on closer inspection it is nothing more than a tree. Or even just a trick of a light. There are a million ways to tell a story. A million ways to burn a bridge.

"He was standing over her,"

What is a child to know about anything really. Especially when the sun burns hot and fierce in the fields, baking the soil and blasting anything in its path. Your vision burns and warps with evaporating water and sweat dripping into your eyes. How are you supposed to see anything when the day is so hot you simply cannot breathe under the stifling weight of the heat.

"What did you see?"

We would not trust a child to run a household, to command an army, but somehow we trust their word more than anything. The eyes of a child are innocent, therefore they must be honest. No one ever seems to consider how dipped in magic our eyelashes are at the age when it comes down to something important, something adult.

"He was standing over her, her skirts were a mess."

He stumbled over the words, hesitance, unsure of what he saw, unsure of how to explain it all. But mother knows and father will make it right.

"Who was he standing over?"

The boy went silent at that. The eyes looked at him dark with some sort of adult emotion he didn't understand. The grip of the fingers on his shoulders is intense, holding him in the swirling wave of emotions crashing over the room.

"Charlie."

The adults in the room didn't need any further explanation from the boy. Quicker than light, conclusions were being drawn and ideas solidified. They knew what happened in those fields, as if they had watched it happen with their very own eyes. The events were solidifying in their minds like stone and it sent a raw and deep panic into them.

The boy's parents needed to get to the Pickney residence, needed to speak with Charlie's parents and needed to make this right.

"Something terrible has happened."

The words were muttered as coats were pulled off of their hooks and hastily pulled onto bodies. Keys fluttered through fingers and fell to the floor, frustrated breaths of air as bodies bent to pick them up. All while the sun hung lower and lower in the sky and lanterns turned on other houses.

Feet moved quickly. Horses moved faster. The boy was clutched to his mother's chest as they rode through their fields fast and hard. A mad desperation clung to the adults. A need to fix, fix, fix. To place a hand over their children's eyes and block them from everything that had transpired the last few hours.

But there was another need that burned a little more desperately than this one. A need to know the truth, to have their suspicions confirmed or denied. Whichever was less painful. They would pry the words from the lips of the children if they had to, if they knew what had happened then they could fix it. They could make sure that it never happened.

"Something terrible has happened."

Charlotte Pickney pushed her bike alongside her as she walked the rest of the way home. There was something wrong with the chain so she hoped her father could fix it. The bike had been her last birthday present and she didn't want anything to happen to it. It had been the best gift she had ever received.

Her pinky was hurting, throbbing with every step she took. She didn't understand why it was hurting so bad she had only scrapped it when she had fallen. Nothing more than a paper cut, but still she had to keep checking it to make sure it wasn't worse. Reminding herself that it really wasn't that bad.

She doesn't remember how she had fallen, simply remembers picking her bicycle up and out of the dirt and continuing her path back home. The sun was beating down on her small body, sweat trickling down her back and making her hands slick. It was so hot that she wasn't surprised that she lost her focus and fell. Maybe she slipped on the sand. It was evidently a great fall by how badly her bike chain had been damaged. She was relieved.

The house was now on the horizon, becoming larger and larger with each step. Maybe Miss Beth would let her take a cool bath even though it wasn't evening yet. She felt sticky and dirty from the heat of the day. Usually the stern woman would say no but surely she would say yes when it was so hot today. There was no way you could do anything in heat like this. It was far too severe to even think.

A little bit of sweat began to fall from the corner of her lip as she rounded the path and began to make the trek toward the shed where she would leave her bike and then to the house. Raising one of her hands while the other remained on the handlebars, she whipped her face. It stung.

Pulling her hand away at the discomfort she inspected the back of her hand. Red was smeared over the back of her hand. Blood. She was bleeding.

And then in a flash she remembers a little more of what happened. Not the fall, not how she ended up on the ground but the moment immediately before she continued on her way home.

Big Willy, massive and terrifying in his posture, leering over which sweat dripped from his face. His hands are simply too close. What had he been doing? Why were her skirts such a mess? Her undergarments ripped? It had to have been him? No one else was there, but Big Willy? Surely he would never betray her like that.

As she reached the front garden of her home, she leaned over sideways, one hand still on her bicycle and threw up everything she had for lunch. The acid burned, even worse on the cut on her lip, but all Charlie could focus on was the thudding of her heart in her chest and the burning cut on her pinky.

Walking to the shed, she placed her bike at the back where it belonged, coughing at the dust in her lungs and feeling a deep set exhaustion begin to take over her. She wanted to bathe and sleep. Maybe a part of her never wanted to wake up and be reminded of what had happened.

She walked round to the back of the house, taking the steps up to the back door and pulled it open. Miss Beth was standing over the stove, working on dinner as she stepped inside.

"Miss Beth, may I have a bath now?" Charlie asked her, her voice soft.

"No child. do your homework and maybe we can squeeze one in-" But as the woman turned to look at her, she froze.

Charlie was standing in the kitchen with her skirts ripped, blood trickling down the side of her face and staining the top of her dress. She had bruises littering her cheeks and mouth area, almost in the shape of a hand.

Her hair had fallen out from its ponytail and was falling around her face but not in a manner that framed her face. The strands were messy and pulled shadows across her skin making her look gaunt and small. At least Miss Beth hoped that they were just shadows and not bruises marring her skin.

"What on earth happened to you?" She said, stepping closer to the girl and grabbing her face in her hands and trying to get a closer look no matter how she pulled away and tried to duck her head. But Charlie didn't respond and didn't say a word. Some stone was overtaking her blue eyes as she looked to the side. Some resolve setting her apart and shutting her out.

She stood as Miss Beth tried to pull the story from the wounds on her face, a sense of horror filling her as she simply didn't know what had happened and how to help the child.

"Mary," Miss Beth called, forgetting her formalities in the moment of stress, "Mary, you need to see this."

It was the footsteps of her mother on the stairs that sent the house into a flurry of action. A gasp, a panic, a phone call. And then several more to follow. Father was called home, her brothers were locked in their rooms, the doctor was called. As the feet ran up and down the stairs, the girl washed and dressed in new clothes, her mother and Miss Beth tried to coax a confession.

Her hair was detangled with consideration from the abrasions at her hair line, her skin carefully washed and taken care of while they searched and looked for other signs on her body. Bruising hand prints wrapping around her wrists, marks distinctly like fingerprints on her thighs and the more they found the more the sour taste on their tongues burned and heavy stones piled in their stomach.

And she sat in the bath with water trickling down her body, letting them move her like a doll, only wincing away when they brushed against her tender skin a little too harshly. But she never protested or said a word.

Somewhere in Miss Beth's horror, the reality of what had happened settled over Charlie and her vocal chords became frozen to a moment, unable to move or regain control. She was stuck, the moment stopping her right there where she had been left. Unable to leave, unable to remember what happened.

"What happened, Charlotte?"

They asked over and over again, softly with the most soothing hum to their words. And she wanted to tell them, and wanted to scream out "I don't know." But there was a stone sitting painfully in her throat, making it difficult to swallow let alone speak. All she could do was sit and look away from their eyes pleading with her to say something, anything so that they could make sense of this splintering devastating turn of events.

"Something terrible has happened."

Was all they could conclude. But what? What had happened? It was an important detail that they missed, something they needed to figure out quickly. All they had was bruises and silence, it was like trying to build a puzzle when half the pieces were missing. They were going off of loose trails and not many facts.

They pulled her compliantly into her night clothes, prepping her to go to sleep. She needed rest, in the morning she would be well enough to speak. The doctor had agreed, placed ointment on her bruises and scrapes and told her not to go to school for the rest of the week.

"All she needs is some rest and she will be ready to talk, she must be exhausted from everything."

But as Miss Beth was pulling back the bed sheets, fluffing the pillows for the ghost of the girl sitting and looking out the window, two horses stampeded into the front garden. A man, a woman and a young boy. The boy was nearly as pale as Charlie as his mother lifted him from the horse and placed him on the ground.

"John, what are you doing here?" Charlie's father called out to his old friend, surprised to see him here and not willing to entertain guests with everything that was burning and churning around him.

"I am sorry to show up unannounced on such short notice Archibald," John began, something rich in his eyes, "But our Michael saw something happen to Charlie this afternoon and we came as soon as he told us."

Briefly stumped at the man's words, he quickly ushered them inside the home and made them too watery tea with stale biscuits. Miss Beth was with Charlie.

But what had little Michael seen in those fields? What had stunned him so terribly that he had to rush home to tell his parents maybe so that they could make sense of it for him. Explain it in a way that he would understand.

He wasn't even meant to run around through the fields, it was too easy to get lost when all of the land looked the same. But he liked how easy it was to run around and be free and often played there after school before his mother came home when he wouldn't get in trouble. His parents never knew of his playground and so he didn't see a reason to tell them.

He had been walking back home then, intent on getting home earlier than he normally would today when he had seen something happening. A person, almost too big to be real leaning over something. He had drawn nearer to them, walked closer so that he could see.

It was the Pickney girl, she was sitting on the ground and the big person was leaning over her.

It was the skirts that had confused and scared him. Her skirts were pulled up and he would see everything underneath. It made him flush red and worry about what his mother would say if she knew that he had seen up a girl's skirt. He wondered then why she hadn't pulled the skirt down.

The whole scene had made him uncomfortable and confused so he had told his parents once they were both home but their questions had just made him even more confused. He wasn't sure of what he had seen.

Maybe he never had been in the first place.

"She's too traumatized for visitors, seeing them might set her off, let's talk to her after they have gone."

Mary had whispered to her husband, from outside her daughter's bedroom with the door ajar. They had gone down stairs and done their best to greet the guests but red worry curled around them, staining their cheeks with panicked confusion and tying stones to their brows as they were weighed down with worry.

"What did he see?" Archibald had asked, looking at the young boy who could only make eye contact with carpet in a room full of adults and unfamiliar energy.

"Go on Eddie," His mother's soft voice tried to pull the word from him as she rubbed circles on his back, "Tell him what you told us."

His fingers twisted together as he opened his mouth a few times before the words began to flow.

"There was a man standing over Charlie," He began, his fingers turning white with how intensely he was playing with them, "In the fields, her skirts were a mess."

The room fell silent with the confession, the adults all watching him carefully, allowing the words to fall into their own truths.

"She looked scared," he said softly. His voice gained its own pitch of fear. His hands stopped twisting as he squeezed them together tightly.

"Who was it, boy?" Archibald asked, his tone tight as a desperate need to protect his family overcame him. He needed a name so that he could put an end to his, swiftly and quickly.

The boy didn't respond, confusion sitting heavy on his face as he continued to look at the carpet.

"Who was it?" Archibald asked again, sterner and loudly.

"I don't know," The boy whispered softly, as he curled further into his mother's side. How was he to know when he didn't even understand what he saw? A moment that he ran from sooner than he had seen. Too frightened to look on for longer.

"Who was it!" The father roared. Protection turning is actions and words desperate, dangerous.

"I don't know!" He cried in response as his mother pulled him to her chest and his tears ran thick and hot and dry. He didn't know, he didn't know what he had seen and certainly didn't know what it all meant. All he knew was that he had to tell someone about the event that sat like cement in his body.

"That's enough Archibald," Mary placated, placing a hand on her husband's arm and urging him to sit down. He stood tall and intimidating, and in no way to treat a child.

"He was a big barn of a man," The little boy said into his mother's clothes but the Pickney's heard and suddenly they didn't need to know, they didn't need a name when the culprit was so simply clear with that description.

And then softer, like he shouldn't say it, "A negro."

"Right," Archibald said as he sat down, determination now over taking his panic. "Thank you for coming," He spoke to the family, "you should head back home now."

The guests were ushered home as the family, once whole and peaceful now a tapestry unwinding, settled in for the night. There was nothing they could really do until Charlie spoke and that would have to wait until morning. So they tried to pull tight, holding on to the quick morning threads of what was once a beautiful artwork.

I often wonder what the little boy thought he had seen. How he had crafted a story from only a moment. How did he know that the glass of water was actually once ice? Perhaps he hadn't, perhaps he never really said anything. But words are nothing with the minds to wield and warp them. All he had done was seen something, and those that he told had filled in everything before and after.

The sunset heavily and painfully that night, a brilliant spread of color like a murder across the sky that quickly turned dark and black with its death. The sweltering heat of the day sunk heavy beyond the horizon and the night turned unusually icy, the winds howling outside my bedroom window, chanting the same words over and over again.

"Something terrible has happened."

But to me, lying there on the floor, pulling the blankets tight and fast around my form it sounded a lot closer to: *"Something terrible is coming."*

***

The morning rose with intensity, light seeping into everything, too early and too soon but ready to take over. Ready to devour. I woke with a certainty that I was unfamiliar with, a sudden knowing that I was awake and sleep was nothing but a memory. A violent awareness of my existence and my body curled and churned with something, a knowing but of what I was unsure.

Even though I woke before I was called, the house was silent, my father, mother and brother had left something that made me feel unsettled. The sun had only just risen and therefore there was nothing that could possibly take their time. But still the house creaked and groaned as the metal stretched and expanded in the onslaught of heat begging to blaze.

I sat in the kitchen, unsure of my next move. I was dressed but stayed clear of making breakfast, I could not control the fire like Mama, best wait until they came back. At that moment I never thought that perhaps they wouldn't come back, the certainty of my home was as strong as the people who lived in it. Nothing could take them or this away from me and that much was certain to me.

So waited, the sky a deep blue and the sun already too hot, it would be a scorching day. And just as I begin to allow myself to worry, Mama and father return but Big Willy is not with them. Mama makes breakfast and I sit and wait, she does not ask me to help like normal. Father leaves again without a word and I am left in my state of waiting. Something will surely come from this. Something will surely happen.

My morning is so different from a routine that I thought would never change that I wait for an explanation or a sudden drop back into normal. Yet my breakfast is placed in front of me and I eat it alone, and then I am leaving home with a confusion that seems difficult to stifle.

"Mama?" I call as I turn before I am truly on my way to school, "What's going on?"

She looks at me for a long moment, for the first time in my life she seems like an ordinary person, "Nothing Child, head on out now." I pause for a moment, watching her carefully but nothing. I will only get scolded if I stay. So I leave.

Even now, I wish I hadn't, wish I had stayed and hidden, listened in on things they thought I was too young to understand. I don't know what happened at my home that day, just as I do not know what happened in the Pickney residence before.

The walk to school felt far too short, my thoughts still scattered and difficult to pick through by the time I reached Black Town. Everything felt too still and quiet even for the early hour and I sat outside the school building and listened to the world wake up. Watching as the residents hurried to their day jobs.

Nothing was said, usually greetings and farewells but nothing to explain the howling winds last night and smothering heat of the morning.

I sit in my class uninterested in the topic Miss Stevens speaks about, my eyes focused on the small window and the strip of sky, a restlessness to know what is going on beyond the walls taking hold of me but I don't dash out. I still have to maintain a level of focus, school is important no matter what is going on outside.

I know there is something happening, the occasional rise of voices making it to the classroom. The sweat on my palms from the too hot of a day. I want in, I need to know.

So when we are let out for lunch, a temporary break from learning before the last two hours of class, I am out of my chair before any of the children and quickly begin to find information.

I stick to my usual methods, ducking around buildings, keeping out of sight all while I listen. I don't hear anything of importance until I catch wind of a conversation that spikes my interest, careful hushed whispers that tip and spill over an open window which I stand near and listen.

"-do you mean?"

"They think it was a sharecropper. They're going to start a manhunt if the person doesn't step forward."

"What reason do they have to believe it's one of us? We ne'er go near 'em. We don't mix with them, we leave their child's alone."

"Well someone had to do it, the girl is in a state they say. The white folk always look to us first, they will ne'er admit that it was one of their own."

I breathe heavily, their own panic mixing inside my body and making my heart race. The voices move away from the window and I can't catch the rest of it, no matter how much I want to know what is going on. What happened? What girl?

But the bell for the school house is ringing and I need to get back. Miss Stevens will tell Mama if I wasn't there for afternoon lessons and so I step back into the building with even less focus. I just want to know what is going on. Want it all to make sense.

I am the first one out when the day's lessons come to an end, I can hear Miss Stevens calling for me but I pretend I am too far to hear. I will bear the scolding tomorrow.

I quickly make it to the edge of town where I need to make a decision, right back home to question Mama until I know what is going on, left for Mrs. Fields to complete my daily reading. I tremble to go home, my entire body pulling me to go that way. I have a deep feeling that I need to be there but Mama will do nothing but send me back. Mrs. Fields may be someone that I consider as a friend but that doesn't make her any less scary. My absence will not be taken well without a proper reason.

So with heavy footsteps and a churning stomach, I begin my walk to Roswell. My mouth feels dry and sticky from the heat but I keep walking. The sooner I get there, the sooner I can be in the cool shade of the living room.

When I arrive in Roswell it is to the same heaviness of something that had been hanging over Black Town. A day of blistering heat and yet it feels thick and heavy with clouds.

I am walking down the main street when I stop and see a little boy standing outside a shop and waiting for his mother. He is a sweet little thing and is looking around him, just taking the world and observing it all. I smile when I see him, such a picture of childhood innocence. A youthfulness clinging to him that I believe I have already lost now.

His eyes land on him and I feel my smile widen. He looks at me hard and squints his eyes together like he is trying to see me better before his face breaks out into a toothless smile. I raise my hand and wave at him and he waves back. The moment tastes warm and rich on my tongue as I feel some of the heaviness of the day begin to slip away from me.

And then he is being lifted up into his mother's arms as she tugs his head to look away from me. She's glaring at me, a rotten look of disgust on her face before she speaks loud enough for me to hear.

"That girl is dangerous, sweetheart. You stay away from the Negro children. They will only hurt you."

The rich taste in my mouth turns dry and chalky and suddenly the atmosphere of Roswell comes rushing back in so quickly I almost choak. I cannot believe the words of this woman. How blatantly incorrect they are or how I could ever be a threat but trying to change her mind will only make things worse.

As she walks away, the little boy watches me from over her shoulder, he pulls a funny face and I try to find comfort in that. The untaintedness of children. One day he will grow up to be like his mother.

I begin to walk down the street and it takes me another minute to notice another change. People are crossing the street to get away from me, they see me coming and then quickly they cross to walk on the other side. Hushing words into their children's ears and watching me from the corner of their eyes like they don't want to lose sight of me for even a second.

I feel the hairs on the back of my neck standing up and even though it is not my normal response, my body pulls into itself and I try to make myself as small as I can. I walk even faster and try not to think too hard about the fact that I am the only one on the street.

Stepping off the main road feels both safe and more dangerous but Mrs. Fields' house is not far and I make it up the steps and am knocking on the door with a pounding heart and head thinking too many things.

I am let in, trying to still myself from my panic but I cannot seem to look her in the eyes. I cannot obey any lessons. Some sense of conditioning I never knew I had is making itself known inside me, a set of rules I have never followed before.

Then, as I read, I was not too loud or too fast but just almost too quiet and without the usual enthusiasm. I didn't think about the lack of commands from Mrs. Fields there at the moment. Or the way her back was rod straight with a mask of control I would never want to associate with her.

If anyone knew what was going on it would be Mrs. Fields. Clearly this was not strictly Black Town business but was rather some kind of warring matter that turned the two towns into countries desperate for more control.

"That's enough for today," Mrs. Fields stopped me with the sun hanging low enough in the sky. Her voice is brittle and showing her age.

I didn't immediately stand to put the book away like I normally would, instead I sat on the stool and stared at the wall for a while before I turned to her and asked, "Mrs. Fields, what's going on?"

She turned to look at me and for the first time since meeting her, she seemed like nothing more than a woman. She breathed deeply and then she said, "I don't know, Child. I don't know."

That sent a true bolt of fear through me, I couldn't even begin to comprehend how she couldn't know when she knew everything sooner than anyone else. And yet she didn't know, couldn't begin to explain it all to me.

"But whatever it is," She added, "It's nothing good."

***

The sun seemed to set too quickly and too slowly all at the same time. For the first time since I began working there, I was grateful for my early departures. I was not sure I would have been able to make this walk in the dark.

It was a violent sunset, the same as it had been the night before. A long afternoon that too quickly burnt up into red, then purple and lastly inky blackness.

I held onto the belief that once I got home everything would be cleared up, an understanding would dawn. Big Willy would tell me if he knew or I could stay up late and listen to Mama and father talk but I would know what was going on by the time tomorrow morning came.

It was a certainty that grew with every step I took right up until the moment it shattered.

Tonight, Big Willy was not waiting for me.

Chapter 6:

Run, Willy, Run

I make the walk home through the fields on my own. Without Big Willy's or Charlie's presence I feel the heat of the day leaving my body quickly, making me draw my arms tight around me as a coldness sets in. I have spent a lot of my youth on my own but this is the first time that I feel alone.

The sun is still setting but the world feels dark and it is made worse by an empty house. The oil lamps have been blown out and no one is around. They were meant to be there when I got back, where are they?

For a long moment I just stare at the door trying to make sense of everything. How I was so easily forgotten and left behind, with nothing to come back to but an empty house. Something is happening, and yet in all the madness, my family could not even wait for me to come home.

I am left behind like a forgotten toy. I don't know where they are or how I am meant to find them.

I remember pushing that door open, expecting it all to suddenly fade like a joke that they played on me but the house was empty and a half made supper sat on the table, waiting for its completion. They must have left in a hurry because Mama didn't even have time to clean up. She hated having a messy home.

Sitting on a stone outside, I wondered where they could have gone and what was I to do if they never came back. The certainty of normalcy was quickly beginning to run away from me and in all the books I read, I could not find an explanation of what to do.

I was so taken by that fact that none of them were home that the thought they may never return did not seem even vaguely to me like an over exaggeration. The consistency of my family did not assure me that they would return. Rather that they would never leave. So if they did happen to leave one day, that meant to me that they would never return.

Deciding that the best thing I could do was seek help in the town center, I began to retrace my steps and then head toward Black Town.

If the townspeople had not been informed of my parents whereabouts then at least they would take me in until such a time as they could come up with a better solution. I was confident in that much.

The sun sunk further and further and I found my eyes straining to see in the dark, an uncomfortable heaviness weighing on my chest with each step and inhale. The dark was only ever safe when I was home, now I was alone and exposed to the world. What terrible thing would this night bring?

I felt so much younger than them, creeping from my room and into my parents bed because the word was too big and scary and I needed the safety of their arms to survive it. Except now I was running into the dark with no assurance of where they were. My stomach flopped uncomfortably inside of me as I clutched my hands together.

I believed, then, that the terrible thing was happening right there in the moment, not that it was the rippling waves of something that had already happened. Now I know, the worst of any event is always the aftermath.

In the center of town there was no light except for in the church building, where the oil lamps lit up the area, calling out to the world around them. And like a moth to a flame, I followed.

It seemed to me, as I squeezed between larger bodies and found a spot that was just breathable near a wall, that the entirety of Black Town was in that church. Adults and children alike all stood there, pressed tightly together and watching the front of the room.

I felt a shiver of anger run through me. Everyone knew of this secret meeting except for me, my entire community was here and yet no one, not even my own parents had taken note of my own absence.

The room was humid with the bodies that occupied it, sweat dripping down the sides of faces, backs of necks and pooling into palms. Everyone was shifting from one foot, faces drawn tight with confusion and murmured words of theories pushing passed lips. The room buzzed with conversation as mothers clutched their children to their chest, tighter, tighter and tighter still.

A fear buzzed through all those present, even I felt it begin to trickle into my body. Something terrible had happened, but in this case not knowing what it was is far worse. No matter how tightly the room was filled, bodies too closely pressed up against each other, you could still see the families drawing clear lines between each other.

Huddle bunches of those that they love, against all the ones that we don't. We were a community in that room, but one that was focusing on protecting their own above all else. I think we would have thrown each other into fire if it meant eternal protection for the ones we held. Tragedy makes you bleed, and when we bleed the only people we want to touch us are those that know our skin.

In the heat and discomfort of that room, I was taken with how alone I was. Everyone in their tight knit groups of loved ones and then there was me. Separated from those I had shared my entire life with and no way of getting to them. Mama was not holding me close to her chest and baring her teeth at anyone who stood even the smallest bit too near. Father did not stand behind us, a force to be reckoned with. Big Willy, well he was not distracting me, he was not making me feel safe. I couldn't see any of them and my gut twisted like a knife with that knowledge.

A throat cleared and the whole room stilled.

"We know that everyone is scared, it's been a long day." It was my father who was speaking, I knew his voice so well but I couldn't see him. Too many bodies for me to see through and over. A mummer broke through the crowd at his words but it was quickly silenced.

I felt an urgent panic to get to him, to be standing beside him. But the bodies around me pressed closer and I felt suffocated.

"We need to work together," Mama's voice now, clear and strong. Before she could continue, a voice broke through.

"They're saying a sharecropper attacked the Pickney girl."

The room turned hotter as people shifted, gasps sprung into the air, everyone had something to say about the matter. The voices were rushed and angry, the bodies were tight and panicked. I watched with concerned and confused eyes. None of what was going on made any sense to me.

Trying to push closer to get to my parents, I felt everyone resist me. Everyone wanted to get closer, wanted to know for themselves what was going on and yet none of us could. I managed to squeeze past a few people but I was still too far to see anything.

"Settle down! Settle down!" My father's voice boomed through the room and every muscle stopped moving.

Heads turning to look at him, ears straining to hear him.

"We understand that many of you are worried, but descending into panic will do nothing but make the situation worse." There was a shuffle, a breath taken by everyone and then Mama began to speak.

"It has been a scary couple of hours, I am sure we have all felt the trouble on the wind," Murmurs of agreement rumble through the church but they settle quickly. Mama has that effect, you listen when she speaks.

"Something indeed happened to the Pickney child, I don't know what but I know that it is serious. They are claiming it was done by a sharecropper working in a field." As she talks, I shift forward, pushing past people. Those around me grumble but they still try to get out of my way, more focused on what Mama is saying than keeping their spot. I can see her now but only just barely. When her words result in another stir through the room, she raises a hand and it stops. A ripple running through the church.

"The people of Black Town are good people," She begins, "We work hard and we stay out of trouble, I know that *if* it *was* any of you, you will do good to come forward but I doubt that it is any of you."

I can see my father and Big Willy too now. Father stands tall next to Mama, a commanding presence that demands all the eyes in the room to be focused on her. But Big Willy is anything but big at this moment. He stands off to the side and further back and he seems so much smaller than he ever has, like his body is folding into himself. I want to run to him, pull him away and hide him but I can do nothing in this moment, except try and push forward.

"The Owners are quick to blame us, the law didn't change that. We may have more protection now but they would still quietly sweep us away if we can. We need to stand with each other, not against each other. We know each other and we know that we would never do this. The owners must look a little closer to each other if they are going to find who did this."

The room seems to settle with every word that leaves Mama's mouth, nodding along to what she is saying and relaxing. The once tight knit groups start to bleed and merge with one another and we are Black Town again, a room full of people who live and die together.

Everyone seems to disperse quickly, I stay pressed against the wall as I wait until the room is empty enough for me to go to my family. When I walk up to Mama and father they look shocked and worried to see me.

"Ruby, what are you doing here? You're meant to be at home." Mama asks me, a scolding look in her eyes.

"The lights were off," I say, "I didn't know what was going on."

"Well," Mama huffed, taking my hand and marching us out of the church, "You should have just waited for us to get back, this is no matter for a young girl."

I bite the words burning in my mouth back, swallowing them with too much saliva. I didn't know if you would come back, I wanted to tell them but they wouldn't understand. Would think I had gone mad. "Of course we would come back," They would assure me, but they didn't understand how unsteadied I had been by the break in my routine today. How much I was troubled by everything.

As we walked through the fields back home, I clung to my mother's hand, trying very hard to ignore how hard it was shaking.

I tried to place everything neatly together in my head. I tried to take what I know and start painting a picture so that I would understand what was going on.

The Pickney girl had been attacked.

That meant Charlie. Charlie had been attacked. But how? And why? An attack seemed like such a foreign concept of brutality. A thing that humans did in the past but no longer touches. I could never imagine hurting something with intention. A person's pain on your hands was a terrible thing.

You would have to be really rotten to accomplish that.

They were blaming a sharecropper.

Did that mean that one of the residents had done it? Hurt Charlie? Or were the white owners only saying it was a sharecropper?

I was missing far too many pieces of the puzzle to try and make sense of it all. Barely even a picture being put together. And still as we walked home one question continued to pound inside my head. *What did it all mean?*

***

My dinner that evening was not soup, rather it was dry bread with molasses spread onto it. The slices were too thick so it made my mouth dry, the molasses too sweet so I was thirsty but I didn't say anything about it. I sat there chewing mechanically as my family was silent. My questions frayed and wound themselves together. When I was finished, I finally opened my mouth.

"Mama," I called but she didn't look at me, only nodded, "What's happening?"

The room tensed and then she smiled at me, one that didn't reach her eyes, "Nothing Child, everything is fine. Head straight on to bed now, it's late."

I stared at her for a long moment and then went to bed. I am sure that my parents have lied to me before but something about this one felt miles worse than any other. It was such a sudden dismissal of everything that was clearly wrong.

Clearly, nothing was fine. My Mama had not eaten and had sat there with too many things for her hands to do and a feeling about her that made me sick.

The meeting in the church was also not fine. I don't understand how they have been able to tell me. Lack of knowledge wouldn't protect me, it would only mean I would be playing with half a deck.

I went into my room, but didn't close the door fully. I didn't sit by the door like I normally would, I was overcome with how tired I was, all the confusion was making me exhausted and so instead, I laid down and pulled my blankets up to my chin and listened.

The chairs scraped on the floor, dishes clattered and bodies moved. They were speaking to one another but it was too low for me to make out what they were saying. But I could feel it, how frantic and frazzled it was.

I was wondering what was happening beyond the door. It sounded like they were preparing for something as they moved around the house. I wouldn't know unless I looked and even then I was too tired to see.

Rushed rises and falls, how it filled me with a sense of dread as my tired eyes stared at the ceiling. They wouldn't tell me a thing it seemed, I was still too young in their eyes. How could I possibly understand any of it?

I would realize the irony of it all later, that the confession of a boy younger than me weighed more than the words of my brother and yet I was far too young to understand anything deemed adult. All because his skin burnt in the sun and mine did not.

I lay there for a long time, unsure what was happening beyond my door but too tired to move. Eventually I fell into an uneasy sleep, my heart beating with the panic outside my room.

***

When I woke in the morning Big Willy was gone. Mama had resumed her usual routine position and father was also missing in action. She didn't mention it, didn't tell me what was going on, just handed me my breakfast and left before I could ask any questions.

My house had once again returned to its empty and lonely state. There was no warmth held within, everyone had left me again with no explanation. I wondered for a moment that if I stayed there, sitting at the dinner table, if time would freeze and I would be trapped in this moment forever. Right where Mama left me with nowhere to go.

I had sat and stared at my empty bowl for a long time, wondering if maybe the pit in my stomach was for silly reasons. Father and Big Willy often left early to go and retrieve supplies, that's why Mama hadn't told me as this was normal. He would be back in the afternoon waiting for me like usual. He had to be.

I ignored the thoughts that wanted to think hard about the panic the night before, the movements around the house that hinted at something more. The rush of fear that had filtered into my room and left the house unsteadily. Those thoughts whispered to me that he would never return and that he was gone for food.

Something terrible had happened, they were blaming the sharecroppers and maybe Big Willy had to leave for a reason. Maybe Mama needed him to get something that would help fix everything.

When I did finally leave the house, I realized that if I didn't hurry, I was going to be late for school. The sun started to hang low in the sky, showing me how long I had just been sitting there without realizing the passing time.

The day moved slowly, like wading through water in the summer heat. I paid little attention to anything and found myself uninterested in the books at Mrs. Fields home. Reading with a vapid voice and then leaving when I was told to. I couldn't hide my need to get home. To make sure that Big Willy was there, that it was just a silly feeling in my gut.

I ignored the looks she gave me. The ones she had when she was trying to analyze and figure something out. Like the truth of everything would be written in their face but I felt that mine was probably more revealing than most. If she knew anything about what was going on in Black Town, she didn't mention it. She just observed me and corrected my reading when she needed to. I was not scolded today for the monotone way in which I read.

I didn't hurry home when I left, no matter how much my feet wanted to rush toward my destination. Big Willy got there at the same time every day, if I was too fast I would get there before him, so I had to walk slow enough that I would meet him there.

But then he wasn't there.

I stood and waited at the crossroads for a long time, hoping that maybe he had gotten caught up in something and that is why he was late. I was so set in my belief that he would come that it took the worry of the night to get me moving once more.

I was alone once more on my walk back to the house, I was expecting it to be dark and my parents absent as well. But Mama was there and waiting for me to return. She got me to help with supper and then sent me to bed straight after washing up. I tried to ask her questions but she simply didn't respond. My worry and anger deepened. I wanted to know what was going on.

***

"Let's have some tea," Mrs. Fields interrupted me in the middle of a paragraph and stood to go and get the tea. I sat there for a moment, wondering why she had so abruptly stopped my reading.

It was the next day and I was no closer to figuring out what was happening and so the time had tickled on slowly all day until I had arrived at Mrs. Fields to do my usual reading. Today I felt her eyes on me even more but tried helplessly to ignore them even more. I wanted her to act normally, her strange behavior was compounding with all the other strange things in my life and making me shift and move uncomfortably in my seat.

A minute or two later, she came back in with the tea and cookies on a tray, placing it at the table and chairs near the window and beckoning me to go over a seat.

Another brick in the routine. Sweat trickled down the side of my face.

"Why are we having tea?" I ask, shifting in the seat I know to be Charlies and looking out the window. Occasionally I get juice and a biscuit during my reading sessions but never tea. I felt more questions that needed answers beat against my skin from inside but I held my tongue.

"Don't bite the hand that feeds you," Mrs. Fields scolds and I stare at her. Unsure of what to do next.

"Drink the tea, Child," She commands gently, nodding to the cup and saucer in front of me on the table. I stare at it for a moment, then watch how she holds it and lifts it to her mouth and imitates her.

I have never drunk tea before that isn't the bitter stuff Mama keeps on the stove all day and makes me drink after supper. When this tastes sweet I am surprised. I take tentative sips, walking the line between wanting to gulp it down and ensure that it lasts forever.

I finally settle on sipping when Mrs. Fields does. The light from the window falling on her face and making her look younger. She must have been very beautiful all those years ago. Her face was like the ones I had seen in some paintings and her sharp and intense gray eyes. I would have liked to have known her then but I'll settle for how she is now.

"You know," She suddenly speaks again, as she places her tea down and turns her focus to me, "I heard a funny little story the other day." Her eyes are playful and there is something, not a smile, pulling her lips up.

"About what?" I ask, copying her posture.

"Well I'm sure you remember Edward Rutledge, he and his friend tried to terrorize you," She starts and I nod, watching her with an intensity that only matches the first day I met her, "Well, he has been walking around with these nasty scratches on his neck."

"Oh," I breathe, I can't come up with an appropriate way to respond to the information, instead I break eye contact with her to look out the window. I don't have any reason to be disappointed and yet I am.

"I heard from my friend that he got into an incident with his horse and in the fall, scratched up his neck," She adds to the story picking up her tea to take a sip, this time she doesn't set it down. I am back to watching her as the room stops for a moment.

"But that's not what I think," She says, peering at me with those same glinting eyes.

"What do you think?" I ask, my tongue is too thick in my mouth.

"I think they looked like someone had scratched up his neck. Maybe one of his victims had really fought back this time." She is looking at me from over the rim of her cup, her eyes saying things so quickly that I cannot begin to understand. Whatever she is telling me, it's important. I simply do not understand why it is so important.

I take another sip of my tea and wonder if she knows about Charlotte Pickney and what happened to her. It feels like Black Town business, something she would not know about but then people had been acting strangely in Roswell since yesterday. She would know, if anyone would.

Maybe I was also wrong about the Black Town business thing. Mrs. Fields craved information, even if it was about people that she was not in contact with every day.

"Mrs. Fields?" I address, sitting up straighter and looking her in the eye.

She smiles at me and sets her tea down, "Yes, Child?"

"Is Charlie okay?"

She's really looking at me now, perhaps if I had known her better than I would have said that she was surprised. Surprised that I knew anything about Charlotte Pickney's state. Maybe she didn't know how Charlie Pickney had everything to do with my strange attitude and behavior the last two days.

She leans back, opens her mouth and then closes it again. She is trying to find the right words to say to me, to explain it all. Finally she speaks

"She's not talking, they can't get her to say a word." I try not to be angry at the lack of an explanation when she keeps going, "Whatever happened to her must have been extremely traumatizing."

I suddenly realized a fact that I had never thought about that maybe this whole thing would leave Charlie maimed just as it was pulling my family apart.

"Will she be okay?" I barely manage to say, my voice only loud enough for Mrs. Fields to hear and no one else.

"I don't know, maybe one day." It's honest and I can't fault her on that. I suppose there isn't a possible way to know whether or not Charlie will be okay.

I didn't know what had happened but for her not to be speaking at all then that means it must be bad. Had I been able to see her I would have been able to see for myself how bad it was but I knew that going to her house would not be fruitful.

I now had more information about Charlie than my own brother, the thought was heavy.

"No one will tell me what is going on." I say more to myself than to the room at large but still Mrs. Fields hears me. Her eyes were watching me carefully.

"I just did," She responds, sitting a little more back in her chair. Something on her face I can only describe as mischief.

I huff out a breath before conceding, "I meant Mama."

Because Mama really wouldn't tell me anything, not again this morning when I was told to eat my breakfast, wash the dishes and hurry on to school. Not when she couldn't even look at me.

Her hands had been shaking when she had handed me my bowl and I tried not to think about that.

She takes a sip of her tea and then places it back on the table, "That's because you are a child."

Those words make anger rush through me once. Just because I am a child does not mean that I cannot understand things. Does not mean I should not be left in the dark. Confusion breeds far worse monsters than reality ever will.

"But-"

"Have a biscuit."

I nearly try to fight her on it again but when I see that she is offering me the good biscuits, I take one and chew it slowly, savoring the flavor on my tongue and how it simply melts into my mouth.

"Why did you tell me?" I ask, still unsure why anything about Eddie should concern me, what it means for all of this. So a child fought back against his bullying. Why should I care? I was glad that he got his neck all scratched up, he deserved more than just some scratches, but it seemed to me like nothing more than useless gossip.

"Tell you what?" She asks in response.

"About Eddie?"

"Because even though you are a child, that does not mean that you cannot think."

And that, that stumps me. All this time, I had never realized that Mrs. Fields saw me as more of an equal than anyone else. I may be young and still naive but she understood that I was learning and growing. That one day my naivety would be wisdom. At least that is what I hoped.

On top of that, I am left fumbling for why this specific piece of information is so important and why I need to have it. What does she think of me? What is she trying to help me work out?

***

I spent the rest of the week waiting outside the door for Big Willy to come home. Waiting to see his beaming smile and massive body move toward me and say; "How was your day, Stone?"

My father returned the night after he left, looking more worn down than I had ever seen him. He had ruffled my hair when he had walked in and then had a quiet conversation with Mama at the stove before going straight to bed. His exhaustion takes priority over everything else.

His return had made me hopeful, I was certain that Big Willy would be back soon and I wanted to be there to welcome him back home when he did.

The sunset seemed to be darker and more violent that week but I was paying attention to them properly and maybe I was just seeing something that I had never seen before. I feel the heat of the day die a quick and violent death, summer seems to have reached its most intense point and will now trickle away into winter as the cold seeps in.

After a week of waiting I decided to break my habit. Clearly he is not coming back. My family had been left incomplete with a missing brother and parents who pretended that this was the way that it had always been. My home turned colder, haunted by the shadow of what used to live in its walls.

Chapter 7:

The Calm After the Storm

I didn't walk down the main road in Roswell anymore.

I had found, quite quickly, an alternative route. It took a little bit longer to get there but it was better than walking down the street and being spat at, having people trip me and mothers whisper in my ear that I was dangerous. The only people that walked on the same side of the road as me were the ones that wanted to try and insult me, making me feel less than due to the richer tones of my skin.

It had taken me a little while to figure out a safe alternative route, but after receiving a mouthful of spit to my face and being tripped so badly that my legs were scraped all down my shins and knees. Walking down main street was no longer convenient, just dangerous.

"Honestly, you would think that they would have the moral compass to at least leave a child alone." Mrs. Fields had muttered while she wiped the spit from my face with a warm cloth. Petunia was cleaning up my legs with an angry look on her face.

"I'll walk her home today Ma'am" Petunia spoke, a motherly softness to her voice that I had never experienced before, "Show her another way where she should for the most part be able to avoid trouble."

"Thank you, Petunia," Mrs. Fields sighed with great relief in her voice.

Usually Petunia left around the time that I arrived but today she had caught me walking up to the house with blood streaming down my legs and a bad limp. She had rushed me inside, desperate to know what had happened for me to end up in such a state.

The tipping had come as much of a surprise to me as my state did to them. A well-timed food had sent my flying to the pavement and then skidding across it for long enough to relieve me of my skin.

I had stayed on the ground for a while, trying to work out what to do or what happened. I was in too much shock for me to feel the pain but before I could get up, I received a face full of spit and the words, "Get out of our town you negro scum."

Slowly, I had pulled myself from the floor, trying not to be too alarmed at the lack of skin on my legs and the blood beginning to peek through. My one leg was in a far worse state than the other and I found myself limping all the way to Mrs. Fields. The pain was so severe that it became a persistent throb that consumed my thoughts and I could ignore all at the same time.

Petunia had stayed with us that afternoon but it had been Mrs. Fields reading and not me.

"With everything going on at the moment, I believe you deserve a rest, Child." So I had listened to her read from a children's treasury in soft tones that nearly lulled me to sleep. When Petunia had decided that she could not afford to leave any later, we had walked out of the house with the sun much higher than it normally was.

Limping down the roads she had told me the route and tried to get me to repeat it back to her a few times so that I would not forget. Pointing out houses to be wary about and what to do if I came across trouble.

"If someone tries to attack you or do anything you run?" She instructed me, "You run straight to Mrs. Fields house as quickly as you possibly can and you don't look back. Scream if you must and we will come and help you."

I nodded my head but that wasn't good enough of a confirmation for her, "Do you understand?"

"Yes, ma'am," I responded, making sure she could see the sincerity in my eyes.

"These folks have no sense of morals anymore, every single one of us negro's are guilty in their eyes," She didn't say the word like the white folk had, she said it with pride. A claim to her identity.

"You're Mama raised you right Ruby, never let your manners and morals go at the expense of how others treat you."

"Yes, ma'am," I responded again and she seemed satisfied.

For all her scolding and strict ways, Petunia seemed to care an awful lot about me and it surprised me. She had walked me right to my house, not just leaving me to part ways once we reached Black Town like I thought she would.

"Thank you for bringing her home, Petunia," Mama had said when we arrived, my blood was beginning to peek through the bandages on my legs now.

"Anything for the daughter of Hattie Mae," Petunia had smiled and then bid us farewell.

"Good grief child what happened to you." Mama said as she pulled me tight to her chest, hugging me with so much warmth and home that I felt like crying. I was used to the treatment from the whites by now but still that day had been too much. A hug from my mama like one I hadn't had in months made me nearly cry.

"I tripped," I muttered into her clothes. She had pulled me back to inspect my face, looking for any other signs of injury. She let out a sigh and ushered me into the house.

That night at supper, my father also had questions, "What happened Ruby?" He asked, his eyes studying and looking down like he could see through the table to the clothes wrapped around my legs.

"She *tripped*." Mama responded for me but there was a hidden message in her words. They shared a look with each other and I looked back and forth between them.

"They're getting bold aren't they, going after children," My father said as he brought a spoonful of soup to his mouth.

"It's only going to get worse," Mama added, and a silence descended on the table. I pushed my soup around my bowl, not wanting to eat it but knowing that food shouldn't go to waste.

"Mrs. Fields wants me to start working weekends," I mentioned the conversation I had had with the older woman a couple of days ago. I felt that I should take her up on the offer, there was one less working body in our family now and we would need to make up for it somehow.

"I told her I would," I finished, taking a large spoonful of soup and not looking up to see my parents' reactions.

With one of the chairs empty at the table, I often found myself unsure of my parents' reactions and responses. Like the missing presence meant that I never know how to behave. I suppose that I didn't.

"That's good, it means she finds you helpful." I nodded at my father's words and ate the rest of my meal in silence.

***

The route that Petunia had shown me was, for the most part, safe. I found which parts to be wary of and how to avoid them so that I could make the passage through Roswell and back safely.

There was the occasional door slammed behind me or slurs and names called through a window but I learnt to just hurry past on my way and not draw attention to myself.

Working weekends added an additional routine to my life that made me relax and breathe for the first time in weeks. A trickly of normalcy flowing back into my life after the world had been turned on its head.

I liked the work, because I didn't read on the weekends. Rather, I scrubbed dishes and floors and then dusted the rooms I was permitted to enter. The work was tiresome and left my body achy but the small envelope of money that Mrs. Fields gave to Petunia to give to Mama once a week was well worth it.

I knew I wanted more than scrubbing floors for my life but I also understood why people did it. You could see the results of your labor in all the layers of dirt being picked up and removed. The work kept all the thoughts in my head silent for once and I was not too troubled by the state of my family and Black Town while I scrubbed the window.

One morning when I had finished all my tasks quickly I asked a question that had been burning in my mind since I had first started working actual jobs

"Mrs. Fields?" I called to the woman who was sitting at the window and wrote what and to who I didn't know but peering over her shoulder, I had learnt, led to a smack on my wrist and a long lecture about respecting privacy.

"Yes, Child," She said without looking up at me, her reading glasses perched on her nose, less than an inch away from slipping off.

"I have finished all my tasks for the day," I began, twisting my fingers together, "and was wondering if I may tend to the garden?"

"The Garden?" She said, turning to look at me, an eyebrow raised.

"Well yes, it's, err-" I struggled to find the correct words without offending her.

"A mess?" She finished for me.

I nodded my head.

"I don't know a lot about plants," I confessed, "but I know enough."

She seemed to be playing with the idea in her head for a bit before she sighed and nodded her head.

"I suppose I'm not going to do anything with it so it wouldn't hurt for you to meddle with it. Just don't turn it to dust," She instructed and I nodded my head eagerly.

I don't know why I had such a desire to work in her garden, maybe because it's overgrown nature reflected nothing of the pristine interior of her house. Perhaps, and this I had not been willing to admit to myself, I was seeking one last connection to Willy when all others had been severed.

I focused on the areas that didn't seem insurmountable, using the tools in the shed that Petunia had showed me with an almost smile on her lips. I began cutting back plants.

With each step I took to get the garden into order, I felt the ghost of my brother hovering around me. His stories he would tell me about the plantations and how to take care of the cotton were loud and clear in my mind.

The more I moved, the more his shadow grew and manifested into something more. Something real. He guided me as he whispered the words of what I should do. At that moment, trapped in the dying heat of a Sunday, there was no Black Town or Roswell, just me and my brother. Escaping from it all.

Tears start to slip down my cheeks, I sit back down on the steps, the garden shears forgotten in my hands and I sob. I cry for everything I have lost, for everything that has been taken from me and for the color of my skin that damns me so brilliantly.

The tears slip down my cheeks like acid and the burn with an intensity that feels almost ridiculous. To cry so pitifully when there are so many things that I need to do. My woe is delayed that it is unjustified but I allow myself the moment of shaking breaths and unceasing tears.

And when my cheeks finally dry, I stand up again and begin to prune the plants.

***

"Petunia and Ruby, I need to speak with you," Mrs. Fields called to us one Saturday as we were beginning to sort out our duties in the kitchen. We both turned to the door before straightening our posture and giving us her full attention.

"I am going to be having some guests over today," Mrs. Fields began, "I need you to prepare the food and tea for when they arrive so you will be doing that this morning." Both of us nodded our heads but then she kept speaking.

"*When* they arrive," She emphasized, "You are not to leave the kitchen under any circumstances until they leave." I frowned not understanding why we would not be serving them like we normally would.

"I will serve them myself and fetch the top-ups when we need them but you are to remain in here at all times, understood?" She asked, her eyes stern and bubbling with something I could only describe as worry.

"Yes Ma'am," Petunia agreed right away but I didn't understand.

"Why?" I asked, looking at her with a confused look on my face.

"Because child," she sighed and looked so much older than I ever thought she was, her features suddenly being weighed down with the reality that had suddenly appeared again. "It is not safe for you anymore, people of Roswell will hurt you if you get the chance, and while I will not dismiss either of you, I will try to protect you as best I can."

I was struck with those words. How was it that I was not even safe in Mrs. Fields' home? A place I had used to escape from everything in my life and had always been happy and content in. A place where I was treated like an equal, like a mind that could think and did.

"This will be the last of my guests for a while." She reassured, realizing that I felt I was losing a safe place for me, "They won't stay more than an hour either."

I had nodded but been fearful of what was to come.

The guests had not stayed long but the tension in the house had made me queasy and unwell. Desperate to escape and get away but remaining quiet and diligent in the kitchen. When the door had closed and I felt the atmosphere ease, I had returned to the front garden and continued my work there.

"Did you plant cotton in my garden?" Mrs. Fields called me.

I turned around, she was standing at the top of the stairs and looking over at me. A long beautiful dress on her body and looking younger once more now that her guests had retreated back to their homes.

"Yes Ma'am." I nodded my head, worried that she wouldn't like it.

She made her way down the stairs and looked around at the area that I had cleared and was not planting up once more. She looked over the cotton plants beginning to grow and frowned, before humming in displeasure.

"Why?"

"The flowers are pretty," I gave as an excuse, twiddling my fingers. She turned her sharp gray eyes on me and raised an eyebrow.

"They were the only seeds that I could get." I conceded, my shoulder slumping down. I wanted to make her a beautiful garden as a thank you but didn't begin to know how.

Much to my surprise, a loud and lovely laugh broke through her lips and she smiled so beautifully at me I was once again reminded of how much she must have stunned people when she was younger.

"Oh you are an interesting one, child," She shook her head and looked over the garden, "You've worked hard and I can see with some seeds the garden will blossom beautifully. I will buy some seeds for the flowers that I like."

I beamed at her words, nodding my head in agreement.

"You will have to wait to plant them though, summer is over now and they won't survive the winter."

I was a little bit disappointed that I wouldn't be able to immediately plant them but I replied anyway, "That you Mrs. Fields."

She gave me a smile and a nod and then headed back inside.

***

Charlie was back to spending her Sunday's with Mrs. Fields but she was different. An air around her that I couldn't pinpoint, some sort of fragility about her that made her look so much smaller and younger than me even though that was not the case.

She was too thin, too pale and too quiet.

Still, she didn't speak, her responses nothing or a shake of the head. Mrs. Fields didn't push her, letting her read or just drink her tea without saying a word to the girl. Sometimes, she would tell her a story but that wasn't often and Charlie never responded. Just continued to stare out the window with those large blank eyes.

Blue eyes had been an envy of mine until now. Hers had gone dull and boring, nothing light or interesting in them. She stared for too long without blinking and they were too dry.

I didn't know what had happened to her but I missed how she used to be, gentle but interesting and kind. Now she seemed to be hardly even a person.

I wasn't really allowed to be around her, a stern look or two from Mrs. Fields was enough to tell me that but I was also simply too busy to really engage with her anyway. A house has a lot of things that need doing once you start looking for them.

So my interactions with the girl were diminished but still I could observe the dark bags that rested under her eyes, the dullness of her hair and the clumsy way she seemed to move when she had once been so elegant.

She also didn't ride her bike on her own anymore. I didn't know if it was just a Sunday thing or it had become her new norm but Miss Beth, the woman that worked in the Pickney residence, walked her to and from the house. Smiling softly when we both arrived or left at the same time but never saying much else.

One morning, just as I was walking up to the house Miss Beth and Charlie were standing outside waiting for something it seemed. I frowned, walked toward them and greeted them politely.

"Good Morning Miss Beth and Charlie," I nodded my head in acknowledgement and both of them had smiled back at me.

"Good Morning Ruby," Miss Beth began, "I have a favor to ask of you?"

"Of course Miss"

"I have something I need to attend to this afternoon and will not be able to walk Charlie back home, do you think you could make sure that she gets home safe?" She asks while resting a hand on Charlie's shoulder. Charlie doesn't say a word or even react at all but still I nod and agree to the request.

"I would be happy to," I responded. Miss Beth looks relieved at my response, she nods her head to me, gives Charlie a hug and then she is rushing off to whatever it is that she needs to do. Perhaps get back to the plantation.

I give one more glance to Charlie before walking up the stairs to the front door, before pulling it open I call over my shoulder, "Hurry, Mrs. Fields doesn't like it when we are late."

I pull the door open and as I make my way to the kitchen to get my instructions from Petunia for the day, I hear her stepping inside and closing the door behind her. The lock clicking into place is the best indicator to me with her silent steps.

The day passes like normal, I complete my tasks without much interaction with Charlie and then when the time comes to head back, she is waiting at the door for me with her head down.

"Good bye Mrs. Fields," I call from the entrance as I tug the door open and step outside. Diligently Charlie follows me.

She doesn't question me when I don't make a trip down main street and instead wind through the back roads. She just walks next to me, so silently that I can't even hear her breathing. A ghost of the girl I once used to know.

After too long of silence I feel awkward and decide to start talking to her. I don't really know what to say so I settle for telling her stories. Silly and strange things about my life and the games I play with the other children. Then there are the stories that I make up, the fantastical worlds that bleed into reality.

I start by telling her how I used to check in one of the sand games that I used to play after school before I started working, realizing as I go that she might not be familiar with the game and having to explain that to her as well so she can follow along with what I am saying.

The story of wits and lies burns into one of the other children that occupy my world and then the words begin to fall like a waterfall and I am telling her anything and everything that comes to mind. The walk home is not extremely long but it is long enough that I babble and chat for an endless amount of time.

I know she is interested by the occasional bob of her head and how she is watching me, not even trying to hide her eyes on my face. Just observing my facial expressions that I so freely give and the occasional throw of my hands when I get particularly passionate about something.

The sun sinks lower and lower and before I know it, I am standing just beyond the path up to her house the point I will leave her to walk the rest of her way by herself. We turn to each other as if it was instinctual and I can't suppress the giggle that bubbles behind my lips.

"You know," I say to her, smiling brightly, "If you ever get bored of reading or drinking tea you can come out and help me in the garden. It's a lot of fun."

Her eyes widen in surprise before she nods and smiles, a little crookedly like she hasn't done it in a while and then is turning to head back inside. I watch and make sure that she gets inside safely and then I am hurrying back home.

I didn't know how much that offer had meant to her, how it made her feel like a human when everyone was treating her like delicate broken glass. Worried that if she even stepped with too much force she would shatter and break into a million little irreparable pieces.

For the first time in weeks, someone was treating her like a person and not an event.

***

The next week on Sunday, Charlie came dressed in pants and a shirt and not her usual dress. I instantly understood why and led her out to the garden where we would work.

I collected all the tools from the shed and then gave her a little demonstration of how each one worked. In sweeping hand motions and excitement, I explained my vision for the garden and what we needed to do to get it there. She nodded a long, listening and then we got to work.

I was surprised at how good of a worker she was. I doubted that she had ever done any real work but she worked quietly and diligently from her spot. She couldn't get through things nearly as quickly as I could but it was still useful to have an extra pair of hands and I was grateful for her help and work.

When she got stuck or didn't know how to do something, she would tug at my dress and point to what she needed me to show her again.

The sun beat down on us but the sweat made us giggle and even happier to work, showing the fruits of our labor on our skin. We were working in the back garden which I didn't realize was intentional on my part until much later. No one could see us or bother us from the back garden.

When midday rolled around, Petunia brought us out sweet, sugary iced tea and we sipped it with contentment and dirt smeared across our faces and we looked over all the work that we had done in the garden. Pleased with how much neater and organized it looked.

When we finished the tea and the thick bread sandwiches that accompanied it, we returned to our work, revitalized and ready to keep going.

Working with Charlie kept my mind off of Willy. It stopped his hands from being so real that they guided mine and stopped his voice from whispering in my ear of all the things that I should do and how to do it.

His ghost was not as present there and my cheeks did not burn with the tears that I couldn't help but shed. My eyes remained dry and I was able to work without everything that my family and town was running from suddenly catching up to me.

As the sun dropped lower in the sky and the shadows grew larger and bolder, I felt Willy's shadow begin to surround me. Looming over me and reminding me that he was still there, some parts of him would never leave.

My eyes strayed to the side and I observed the other ghost of my life, one that had been created on the same day as Willy. I wondered if she felt him as I did, his presence all around. Both safe and terrifying all at the same time. Reaching out and trying to get to me no matter what.

I wonder if it looms over her too.

Chapter 8:

Hide and Seek

Winter was well on the way now, the mornings being tight and cold, the evening's dipping quickly into darkness as the sun set earlier and earlier each day.

Food around the house had surprisingly been better. It seemed to be the only thing that had gotten better in recent months. I heard Mama mentioning to Papa that Mrs. Fields paid me well for my work on the weekends and so we were able to afford a few more luxuries.

Getting them, however, was another story.

The shops had slammed their doors to the residents of Black Town. We simply were not allowed inside, large signs outside the buildings clearly indicated that they were only serving white customers.

Not that it was safe to walk down main street anyway. Too many people willing to take their anger out on anyone who walked too close. Who drew too near.

The incidents of tripping and spitting did not start and end with me. Many of the children came back from errands for their parents with split open knees and bruised skin. The adults were also not spared. Their clothes ripped in tassels, bags stolen from them or spit dripping down their cheeks. There were very few residents of Roswell who still treated us with care and kindness.

The supplies and resources in Black Town had dwindled without access to the shops in Roswell. Without access to the main town, there was a need to seek supplies and resources but the next town over was quite a bit further, about three hours if you walked. The family that ran the general store made a big trip to the town once a week but people were starting to struggle with the lack of supplies. No way out of our predicament.

Some of the men in the town were going to try and get a house and cart by pooling some money together so that they may be able to bring more stuff back with them and make the trip a little quicker. Still a real solution had yet to be found and so we bartered and exchanged to try and keep everyone fed and safe.

A level of despondency had fallen over the town, many had lost their jobs in Roswell as the fear and panic of the whites had spread. Women who had been working for families since before the children were born were now a danger and a threat. Men were far worse, no longer able to take on odd jobs here and there as there were far too many risks. They wouldn't let us stain their streets.

There were a handful of us who had been protected from the purge, remained in our positions and worked because our Mamas believed that we were still good people, that our race didn't define us. Petunia and I were safe, Mrs. Fields had a lot to say about the attitudes of the people of Roswell and none of it was good.

"You and your families need this work now more than ever," She had said to us one afternoon while we were stopping to have lunch, "I will not abandon you simply because of a situation no one truly understands. Fear is not my commander."

Petunia smiled at her gratefully, "Thank you, Ma'am."

"Thank you," I spoke as well but softer and less sure of yourself.

"However," She said, "If coming here starts becoming a true threat to your safety and I am not positive that you can make it here and back unscathed then I will terminate you services until such a time as this all blows over."

There were others who hadn't lost their jobs and Petunia made friends with them all so that we could walk to and from work together.

"Safety in numbers." She had told me when I had found a group waiting outside the house one Tuesday afternoon.

I had found it rather amusing that most of the women who retained their jobs worked for families or people on the same street as Mrs. Fields. It seemed to be the sane street in Roswell, one that remained without prejudice or an intention to cause harm. According to the other women of Black Town, many of them were friends with each other and constantly had talks and meetings to discuss the apparent illness of mind that had overtaken the town.

I was grateful that I had an escape when so many people were struggling to stay afloat with all the changes and hostility.

"The lack of food is making people panic," My father spoke up as we ate, the bags under his eyes dark and deep. The town had turned to my parents for guidance during this time and they were beginning to struggle with their options and what more they could do.

"Food is a necessity," Mama agreed, "There isn't much we can do without it. They should have the cart by next week which will help."

"Still, everyone is getting more and more scared and it's making them irrational." Father added looking at Mama with dark eyes.

"We haven't been the most level headed either," Mama reminded him. I didn't know what they meant by that, they seemed relatively calm for the most part but I was often shut out and hidden away then things got too intense, a means of protecting me.

"We can try-" my father started but was interrupted by a knock on the door. All of our heads turned to the door wondering who it could be at such a late hour.

Standing up from his seat my father moved to answer the door, mama and I watching from behind him. When he pulled the door open none of us were expecting to see who was standing there.

"Archibald Sir." My father greeted, surprise clear in his voice, "What can I do for you this evening?"

Archibald Louis Pickney III was the owner of the Pickney plantation and a very honorable man. He had been the first in our area to open his plantation up to sharecroppers, the first one to take him up on the offer had been my father.

He was a short portly man with a balding head. He wore spectacles on the tip of his nose and I had often heard from Charlie that he would say he had lost them only for them to be on his face.

He was kind to his workers and approached them like business partners, they had a say on the operations of the plantation and were not just workers doing his bidding and listening to his every command. They had autonomy, something very few did.

He was very clever and ran his plantation well. I could admire him for that even if the first time I met him soured his personality in my mouth considerably.

It worked in his favor. His plantation was one of the most successful around with a high yield and very diligent workers. There had never been an issue with him and my family, we coexisted peacefully. Until now.

"Good evening, Tobias," He greeted formally but he did not make a move to shake my father's hand like he normally would. He just stood for a moment before speaking.

"We have worked together for many years, Tobias, I have respected your decisions and you mine. In a different time I may have even called us friends, but things are changing now." The man let out a sigh and I watched him from behind my mother. Taking in the stiffening of his posture.

"Where is William?" Archibald demanded. My mother tensed in front of me.

"I don't know, Sir." My father responded easily, Archibald looked angry, upset about the whole demeanor and response of my father.

"I understand that you are trying to protect your loved ones but your son must be punished for what he did. The panic and fear will only get worse if he doesn't." Archibald tried to coerce my father into speaking. Threatening the hell fires to only grow hotter than they already were.

My father, however, stood there and looked on like an unyielding rock. He did not waver and did not cower underneath the man, just waited.

"Goddamn it Tobias," Archibald snapped, reaching up and grabbing my father by the collar of his shirt, "Tell me where he is, tell me where he is right now or I swear to god-"

I was hiding behind Mama now, terrified of the rage and heat radiating from this man. It was making me nauseous, its intensity. But my father was a big man, not quite as large as Willy but still built like a bull. Taller and stronger than Archibald. He reached up, wrapped his hand around his bosses and then removed his fingers from his clothes and took a step back.

"My son is not the man you are looking for. I don't know where he is but I know that he is safe from all the lies and falsehoods that are being spread around here. If you were not so quick to blame the people who have always served you, maybe we would help you find the real criminal." My father spoke with clarity and an unwavering confidence.

"Someone has to pay!" He roared, "My daughter is a mess, she is so broken by this, this monster that dared lay a hand on her and I have to make them pay."

His cheeks shone a radiant red, for a moment I wondered if he would start crying.

"I agree," My father nodded, "But that monster is not my son."

"Somebody saw him."

"Who? A child? A child who saw something that he didn't understand. A moment that can be taken out of context." It was Mama who was speaking now, holding me tight to her back, with my face pressed into her clothes I can feel how she is trembling.

"That child didn't know what he saw. You created the story from his confession, you turned a moment into a crime. Until Charlie speaks up, you are not touching our son." Mama said.

"You will pay for this Johnson," The man screeched, "You. Will. Pay. I will burn your son when I find him for what he did. I will burn him!"

My father closed the door in his face and the man stormed off. I could hear his heavy stomping feet in the sand and then I felt the whole house take a deep breath.

My parents were reeling with the knowledge that their livelihood and safety may be taken from them very soon and I was weeping. Weeping for a man driven so desperate that he could no longer think.

His fit of rage, although uncomfortable and horrifying initially, had not made me scared of him in the end. Only sorry that he seemed to be even more broken than all of this then we were. Charlie may be hurt, but he clearly didn't see her the way I did. A someone who was slowly but surely knitting herself back together. Finding a way to live and make it through it all, despite what had happened to her.

"We're in trouble now." Mama whispered and pulled me into a hug. She had been giving them to me a lot lately, like she worried it may be the last one she ever would.

***

Church on Sunday was a disaster. There was a cacophony of yelling, children crying and all out just noise.

I had been sitting in the front row since we had arrived with my hands clamped firmly over my ears. My parents had been trying to gain control so that we could work through some things rationally. But people were angry, furious that things weren't getting better, that we were being punished for the sins of another.

As the noise and crowd shrugged forward, my mother picked up a stick and began to smack it against the podium. The sound makes everyone calm down and silence themselves. Order finally falling on all of us.

"I know yer all scared and tired but screaming and making a mess of things ain't gonna help no one." She called out to everyone, catching their attention and bringing the focus onto her.

"I know that we are facing difficult times, I know that you all want an answer but the truth is I don't 'ave 'em." A mummer ran through the church but she kept speaking, turning the eyes of anger to ones dipped in the blue of sympathy.

"My son has been declared a monster when he was doing nothing but trying to help. My son is a good boy, I had to send him away to protect him until we find who really did this. There is nothing any of us can do until the girl talks." She breathed a heaviness on her shoulders I had seen growing heavier with the passing weeks.

"So what do we do," Someone called, a murmur of agreement followed.

"We make provisions," The pastor began, speaking for my parents, "The cart arrived this morning so the food situation should improve. Some of the women still working in Roswell are going to get their Mistresses to buy whatever we cannot get. We work and we survive and we pray that the good lord will guide the young girl to truth."

There was a moment of silence, I took a sharp intake of breath and waited for the building tension.

"And what if she doesn't?" someone asked. Everyone turned to see who had spoken, I tried to see over the sea of heads.

"What if she doesn't speak up, it's only going to get worse for us." The people next to me shook their heads and pulled tighter, before Mama, father or the pastor could say anything someone else spoke.

"If she hasn't spoken in a month," They began, "Then we tell 'em where Big Willy is hiding."

Gasps and words of agreement ran through the church, Mama turned pale.

"It doesn't matter if they find him or not," My father began, "If the girl doesn't speak they will still keep coming for us. Taking Big Willy will only satisfy them for so long. If it's not a proper confession then everyone is guilty. We have to wait for the girl to confess."

I could see it in the room. The lines being drawn in the sand. How everyone was breaking up and siding with one or the other. The parents who knew my parents were right, and the ones who wanted all of this to end. Would turn against each other if it meant getting it.

It was like setting a game up to play with the other children, the lines needing to be clear and bold so that we would not lose them in the roughness of play. Sides were taken and chosen, everyone with the goal of winning. Black Town was splitting down the middle before my very eyes and I was falling to neither side. Stuck somewhere on the line with no place to go.

We had always been united, never separated. A community looking out for each other. But here we were, choosing sides all because of something terrible, the actions of one person changing so many lives and damaging so many relationships. I didn't know what to do sitting there in that church. Scream maybe.

About how stupid everyone was being, how unfair and unkind this all was. I wanted to scream at all those adults who thought they knew better. But I was a child and they would see my wisdom as a tantrum.

But more so I didn't believe my parents that my brother had run off to protect himself. He ran for himself, no one else. If he was hiding for protection then he would have taken me with him. He would have looked after me rather than leaving me to pick up the pieces of his disappearance in a broken town with broken people.

Big Willy always made sure that we stayed together so he would have kept me safe first. He never would have left if he could have done something about it. When he could have fixed it.

He left for himself and I found that I was furious with him. For running, for hurting our parents and for leaving me. Leaving me in a town I never wanted to be in, for running away when it was the only thing I had ever wanted to do.

He left me behind and he didn't even think about it twice. Maybe he had run to protect himself, maybe he really was in danger but in my rage and hurt I was struggling to see the act as anything other than selfish.

At first it had seemed to make perfect sense, he had gone and he would be back. It would be alright in the end.

Big things, big emotions and events, take time to work out. You often don't know what you feel in the moment because you simply don't feel it. You are running too much too soon and then as it all filters away you can understand what it is you feel. I was angry, furious that he left me. I didn't know how to save my family, I didn't know how but it felt like it was my responsibility.

***

I knew I should have left straight to Mrs. Fields. She didn't like to be kept waiting and there were a lot of things she needed me to get through today but I had seen Mama and father talking behind the Church and my curiosity got the better of me. I had to know what they were talking about.

I creeped down the side of the building and then peered around the edge to watch them.

They were speaking in hushed tones so I couldn't make out what they were saying to each other but that was not what left me so taken aback and a panic in my chest.

It was Mama, I had never seen her like this.

Her cheeks were coated with tears and there was a deep rooted panic and fear in her eyes. They reminded me of a wild animal, like something was threatening her life and she had no way of defending herself or stopping it from happening. All she could do was fight like a caged animal and hope for the best.

I had never seen her so distressed. Mama and Father always knew what to do, they had a way out of things. It was the way I found them to be special. Here in the moment, with my mother's tear stained cheek and panic filled eyes, I was realizing the intense humanity of my parents. They were people just like me and they didn't have everything figured out.

They didn't know what to do about *this*.

My father gripped my mother by the shoulders to try and steady her in her hysterics but I wondered if maybe he too needed the steadying. That he was just as worried and distressed as she was. I couldn't see his face but I could hear how his voice wavered and strained against the strength of his own emotions. He also didn't know what to do.

I think they had been weathering the storm and then Archibald had arrived last night and now they truly were afraid. They hadn't wanted me to see it, and had acted calm while I was still in their line of sight. But now the emotions were bubbling over, they couldn't contain it and this moment was a result of that stress.

The humanity of your parents is a difficult thing to comprehend and understand. They are meant to be extraordinary but everyone falls from grace at some point.

Their own fear didn't make me feel afraid or panicked like I thought it would but rather I was left feeling consumed by my helplessness. There was nothing I could do to comfort them.

I choose to stop intruding on and stealing their moment from them and left to go to work. We can only do so much, this was one thing that I could do.

***

My Sunday with Mrs. Fields after the discussion at the church seemed to fly by. I was not able to throw myself into work and stop thinking like I normally was. No matter what I did or how hard I worked my mind kept going back to the situation at home and my missing brother.

I seemed to be stuck in Black Town and my usual break was more tormenting me than it was helping me. I left out a huff as I stared at the bathroom floor singing the expressions of my parents swirling in the tiles and hearing their words with every scrub of the brush.

I wiped the sweat on my face and wished, not for the first time, that I could run away.

My pouring thoughts meant that the day rushed past me and soon I was packing up the last of the cleaning tools before heading out the door with Charlie and a call over our shoulders that we would be safe.

We walk in silence, for the first time I cannot find the energy within me to rattle on about my thoughts or tell the girl stories. I want to distract her and make her feel happy as I know she rarely gets it now but I am so full of anger and fear that my stories and voice will do nothing but make things worse for her today.

She still doesn't speak or make much of a sound really and I find myself desperate after this morning in the church. She *has* to speak. I need her to speak more than anyone.

I don't push her, I don't know if I could say anything that would make her understand or push her to speak when her own family has not been successful with that attempt. I cannot do anything to make her talk.

Still, as I walk beside her I brew in all emotions of bitter and sour. The intensity of them can be felt on my tongue, dancing along my tastebuds. Sickly sour lemon, so intense that it burns and makes my mouth feel numb. A desperation like no other. The bitter, I'm not sure what exactly, maybe the bitterness of the rind after the peel. It's so bitter that it coats the back of my throat, clinging to it and reminding me of bile. Anger.

I want to be peaceful and calm. I want to be rational and think of clever ways to fix all of this but the rug underneath my feet keeps being tugged over and over again and I am struggling to stay on. Struggling to balance myself. It makes me irrational and floundering in my actions and attempts.

And Charlie. Charlie seems almost at peace with her state, like she has accepted it and moved on. She had no urgency to fix any of this, no need to confess to what happened. To clear my brother's name if he is guilty. She *knows* it couldn't have been him. Whatever it is, Big Willy is a good man. Willy would never do anything to hurt someone, he would never do anything wrong. Charlie *has* to know that, because she knew him. She might have even known him better than I did.

Children are often less naive than we think they are, I was sure of that, but the one thing adults are right about is they are often not the best at looking beyond the surface. They aren't as good at picking apart facades as those who have been hurt by fake appearances and have to look carefully for them. Of course children are much better at listening to their feelings, they know when something is wrong. I knew something was wrong with Charlie, I could feel it, but the longer she wore that mask of okayness the more I began to believe it. To some extent I believed that she was over it all, she had passed.

How was I to know about her waking nights with sweat clinging to her night gown as her brain screamed at her to get away. To run. From what she could never remember, it always seemed to slip from her right as stepped into the waking world. She could remember the terror, the desperation to get away or be saved but from what or who she did not know. The only thing she could remember upon waking were the deep, rich eyes of Big Willy and no knowledge of how they got there and into her dreams.

She would wake with a broken exhaustion, too terrified to fall asleep to be plagued by her nightmares once more but too tired to even fathom staying away. She would lie there, staring at the scene, wishing her mother would come into her room and rock her back to sleep like she was six again and the world was too big with too many shadows.

Sometimes, on the really bad nights when her tears were too thick to see and her breaths too fast to breathe, she would stumble and fumble out of her bed and down the hall. She would sneak into her little brother's room and into one of their beds and hold them tight to her chest, reminding herself that they were safe. Here, in this room under the protection of the blankets, nothing could touch them. Dreams were still just dreams even if you had lived through them.

I could see none of this on her face. We wear our demons in our hearts after all.

I stopped suddenly realizing that Charlie was no longer walking behind me. Turning around I saw her stopped and looking down as something on the ground. Walking up to her I noticed that there was something shimmering gold in the sand. She stared down at it and I looked at her questioning.

"What is it?" I asked but she only shrugged.

Slowly she bent down and picked it up, shaking it to get most of the sand off and then dusting it to make sure that there was nothing on it. Turning it back and forth in her hands, I could now see that it was a small, round golden object with a button on the top. The face was intricately patterned with swirling filigree engravings that reminded me of weaving vines or even cotton branches.

Engraved on what I presumed to be the front was the letters *LTD*.

She clicked the button on top and the lid popped open to reveal a watch face.

"A pocket watch," I say and she nods her head, dragging her finger across the face and staring at it with so much intensity. As if it could speak to her if she looked at it hard enough.

It's a beautiful pocket watch, nothing like the practical ones that some of the sharecroppers have to keep track of time and nothing else. This is a rich and beautiful display of wealth, made even greater by it being dropped into the dirt.

"We need to keep going," I say, "The sun will set soon."

She stares at the watch for a moment longer before clutching it tightly in her hand and following behind me, silent as ever.

We are not far from her house now. I feel that bitter acid in my mouth gets even more potent. When we stop at the point, I always drop. I can't help myself any longer.

"I know you have been through a lot and must be really scared about everything," I begin and look deeply in her eyes, "But this is not just affecting you. You are not the only one hurting by this. Willy is innocent. I know that you know he is."

My voice sounds pathetically desperate to me but I don't care right now, her eyes are looking at me with a deep confusion and concern and it does nothing if not make me want to scream.

"Please Charlie, I know that you know Willy would never do that. He would never hurt you. He was your friend!" I exclaim with tears welling up in my eyes, "He's always been good to you so be good to him too. Tell them what really happened."

She is looking at me with a blankness now, a detached disinterest as the tears in my eyes get too much and spill over, running down my cheeks hot but I ignore them and keep going, "Just tell them what happened and everything will be okay, if you just speak. That's all you have to do. I promise it's easier than breathing."

"I just want him to come home, I just want my brother back." I am full on sobbing now and Charlie does nothing but stare. My hands are clutching onto her shoulders as I stare at her. Shaking her as my body quivers and shakes with my need.

"You're the only one who can do it! So you have to! You have to bring him back, you have to tell him that he is innocent Charlie. Please Miss, please tell them that he is innocent."

I feel myself descended further and further in my panic and fear as I mutter over and over again *"bring him back"*. The words are barely coherent as I fumble over them and snot drips from my nose onto the ground below me.

Slowly, Charlie reaches up and removes my hands from her shoulders. Without looking back at me or saying anything to me she walks away and up toward her house. My sobs reach a new fever and I choke on the air in my lungs, my last chance of home walking away from me as I stare after her.

What am I supposed to do? No one will listen to me. No one will believe me and yet they believed that little boy. They believed that boy because it was convenient to them, but I was nothing but a Black child too close and yet too far away from it all. There was nothing that I could do. Nothing that I could say to change it all.

What am I supposed to do?

Chapter 9:

Memories Disguised as Nightmares

It must have been the heat. During the hotter months the soil on the farm became more sandy for lack of moisture. It meant that the roads she usually could fly down on her bike with the wind in her hair now had to be walked, pushing the bicycle next to her.

Sweat trickled down the side of her face, her clothes feeling sticky and uncomfortable from a day spent in the hot air and the journey back home in the sun. She had slung her book bag into the basket so that it did strain her shoulders down but how it was making the front of the bike drag in the sandy soil.

She wasn't far from home, nearly the homestead on the plantation where she lived. Usually she liked the walk through the fields, she could take to some of the workers and if she was lucky she would get to have a chat with Big Willy.

"Hiya Charlie," the voice was chipper and stopped her in her tracks. She looked around and saw that it was

Eddie and Tubby. She smiled politely and gave them a slight nod of her head.

"Hello."

"Wher' ya headin'?" Tubby asked. His voice a little softer, a little easier to listen to.

"Home." She smiled politely again and shifted her feet, she would rather that this conversation ended soon. Tubby and Eddie left her feeling uncomfortable, she would often find ways of getting away from them as quickly as possible.

"Ah well," Eddie began, taking a step toward her. "That's nice." His smile was crooked and pulled in all the wrong places, "Why don't you come to my family's plantation for the afternoon."

A cold shudder runs down Charlotte's spine at the thought of spending an extended amount of time with the two boys. She couldn't bear the thought of a few hours with them, she isn't really sure what they would even do.

"Oh," She forces a smile toward them. Her Mama always taught her to be polite, "Thank you for the offer."

She shifted her grip on her bicycle and tried to not look like she was going to make a run for it at any given opportunity. They had that effect on people, Eddie and Tubby, making you want to leave as soon as you had arrived.

The boy's smiles had seemed too broad to her, too stretched and not like the soft sweetness of her mother. Or the youthful joy of her brothers.

"But I need to be getting home," She dismissed. It wasn't a lie, her Mama had asked her to 'hurry back straight' and she didn't want to keep her waiting. "My Ma needs me this afternoon."

"Oh well maybe another time then," There was a tinge of something in Tubby's eyes that she couldn't understand, a smile on his lips that didn't seem to be linked to happiness. She quickly nodded at them and then began to walk away, wheeling her bike behind her.

It takes a lot of force to knock someone out, more than you often think. People are strange like that, they can take everything and nothing at all. They must have hit her hard, must have really been desperate to do that sort of damage.

She told me about it years later, that of everything she remembers the rock hitting the back of her head better than anything. How blistering hot and instant the pain was. How her whole body went numb with it and the force threw her to the floor. How her eyes screaming in whites and Black people and her vision turned to a wobbly soup. How desperate she wanted that pain to vanish.

"It makes you silly," She had said to me with a faraway look in her eyes, "You want to get away, your brain knows that you are in danger but you can't move. You're simply in too much pain."

You must be a very blackened sort of person to be able to hurt someone like that. To maim them.

It was a hand on her ankle that snapped her out of the dizzying spin, the swirling mix her head was in. her body being jerked backward that reminded her that something was terribly, terribly wrong. Her body started to be dragged backward in a jerking motion and the force of it caused her head to hit the ground but it was enough for her to open her lips and scream.

Kicking her legs out behind her, she started to desperately try and get away from the attacker. Eddie and Tubby she remembers, her brain struggling to process and think in the heat of the moment but desperate to try and get out of the situation. If she was a bit more lucid maybe she would be able to digest her horror.

Her feet kick wildly, desperately trying to connect with something, the further she is dragged away from her bicycle. Her foot manages to connect with something, a grunt is hurt before a voice calls out.

"Hold her down, Tubby." Eddie doesn't sound like she has ever heard him. His tone is so dark that it sends a shiver down her spine, a vicious side to him that she had only seen glints of in the past. She never expected *this*.

Before the instructed hands are able to get a grip on her she manages to turn around and reach upwards. Eddie is leaning over her, his body seeming larger and stronger than it ever has before. Like a towering beast trapping her in. In a blind panic, desperate to do something before she was restrained further, Charlie began to scratch at the boy. Her fingers leaving deep ridged marks across his skin and scarring him of his misdeeds. The lines are ugly and look like they burn but apart from launching an even deeper rage into his eyes, it does nothing to deter his intentions.

Her hands are pulled away from him and pressed together. The motion is violent, every muscle in her body protesting the movement. But the rigidity is futile against the attempts and all it does is make her burn from the force being exerted. Her hands are held behind her back as her upper body is pushed into the ground, her mouth filling with sand and putting an end to her screams and cries.

A meaty hand pushed against her lips but it is pointless as her mouth is dry and too dusty for her to get a sound out as she sputters and chokes on the feeling. Heavy with the resolution that there is not much she can do to prevent the situation, her eyes sting and burn. Charlie can't decide whether it is because she is trying too hard to cry, a refusal to give them her tears if they have already stolen her body or if it is the dust that's doing it. Perhaps it is somewhere in the middle.

A hand moves along her legs, barely there but hot and too close. Disgustingly close. It takes her a minute but when she feels the hot and dry summer air meet her skin she realizes that he was pushing her skirt up to rest above her hips. She screams into the hand and the dirt, the last of her fighting will break loose and be snuffed out by the bruising grip on her body.

The steady beat of her heart in her eyes is momentarily broken by the sound of fabric ripping. Her eyes burn even more intensely. She is exposed and she can't fight back. Nothing she will do will be able to throw the two boys off of her.

In a moment of brief waning in the pressure on her body, she is able to turn her head to the side, her left cheek pressed into the sand, raw as it rubs against the broken glass like grains.

Lying in the sand a little away from her face is a pocket watch. Its bright silver exterior speaks of money and care, it is clear that it is a loved item. Polished to perfection and not a single mark to indicate that the owner doesn't love it.

"Who would just drop such a beautiful thing into the sand like that," Charlie had said to me. Her anger was raw and hot, the intensity of it a little frightening if I didn't know how justified it was.

It seemed to have stuck with her, that pocket watch. How something so tenderly looked after could be tossed aside in a moment of devilish acts.

It shimmered in the fading afternoon light, its glint warm when her whole body felt cold. Had she been able to, she would have reached a hand out to touch it. Grasp its shimmering coolness between her fingers and root herself to reality. Remind herself that in moments like this, there were still beautiful things.

Charlie didn't know what was going on behind her, the conversation or actions being committed. Maybe she would let her mind pull up the images months later. The look on their faces. Were they smug? Or Angry? Did even a dust of guilt sweep across their features. But then, lying in the sand, all she could do was to will herself to not think. As the first salty tear slipped from her eyes, hot and burning.

As it dripped down her nose, clearing a path from the dirt that was once there and staining her face with the memory. It fell to the dry earth that greedily ate it all up. Desperate for any kind of moisture, even that of fallen grace.

Her body shifted, pushed deeper into the ground, she felt another tear fall. None of it mattered anymore, she desperately wanted it to end.

Someone. Please.

"My mind was begging for a savior, one that ne'er was gonna come." Her words flew away with the wind. The tragedy in them is heavy and full of grief. The soft skin under her eyes seemed to turn blue with the heavy weight of remembrance.

Had I not known better I would have tried to hug her but she had been touched enough and would never need foreign hands on her body ever again. She could go a lifetime without it.

The pocket watch had the initials *LTD*.

A moment of time moving through the seconds thick like honey was suddenly flushed with hot water. The sweaty hands that had been pressing bruisingly into her skin were pulled from her body and she was able to move.

There was a scuffle behind, that she could hear but it was muted, like someone had shoved cotton wool in her ears. The sounds of kicking and shoving and a raw powerful scream. Not one of fear or panic but raw rage and fury. A dragon that had its treasure stolen from it.

Some sounds were more raw than others, the sound of skin hitting skin and then the thundering of feet as they ran to get, leaving a spray of sand to get into her eyes.

Slowly, like her body had forgotten that it had autonomy over itself, Charlie began to pull herself up off the floor she had been thrown to, rolling onto her back the first thing that she noticed was the vast and bright blue sky. She could still hear yelling, and more running but the sky seemed far more important.

It was so wide, open and blue. So blue that it seemed untouchable in that moment. Not even a cloud could taint it, it was completely and utterly free. Not trapped on the ground with sand in its eyes.

Her ears were ringing, with blunt force trauma or perhaps the raw, intense fear. There was something underneath the chanting bell in her head, yelling she supposed but it was all wrong. Like when you hear a conversation from under your comforter. It's wobbly and unintelligible.

Charlie lifted her head from the ground, her eyelashes and lips dusted in sand and dirt. Her mouth feels dry and warm, like she said too many things too quickly. She wants to sit up, but she's afraid. If she sits up won't she only be pushed down again? Is this not some elaborate game? Another way to torment her?

But the scuffle, the hands being ripped off her body. Did somebody save her? Did somebody hear her cries and fear and come and protect her? Throw the boys off her?

When she finally does dare to look up, it's to see the dark brown of Big Willy's eyes staring back at her.

His body feels large, towering over her. Sweat drips down his face as he struggles to catch his breath.

He rests a hand on her shoulder, helping her to stop swaying from side to side. There is concern in his eyes, a sort of panic she had never thought would ever be there in his innocence.

"You're alright Miss?" He had smiled, all sweet and boyish, "I threw them off you Miss Chased 'em bad seeds away. Eddie and Tubby are gone, Miss Charlie."

Maybe it was the soft way he was speaking to her, or the reassurance that whatever she had just gone through was over but she had wanted to cry. Wanted to sob and scream.

Her mind was hazy, breaking up into pieces, the longer she just sat there and stared at his face. The moments began to slip from her, her brain desperately trying to get away from it now that it was over.

"I had been so confused then," Charlie had spoken, her voice shaking with something, "I didn't understand what was going on and he was the only thing I could latch onto. The boys had already run off. Even when I remember it, I can still remember how confused I was. How I didn't understand that it was Willy. In the pain of my confusion, I felt betrayed."

Part of me had wanted to ask her what she had been thinking. Big Willy was the best sort of person, no one should ever suspect him of such a thing. He wasn't capable, he simply wasn't. It made me angry to think that she ever believed that he could do such a thing. But confusion muddles you, it makes you all messy inside and you can't think straight.

Reaching down, Big Willy grabbed her hands and pulled her to stand, moving her dress so that she was covered. She was shaking like a leaf in the wind as he tried to walk her to her bike. Her betrayal tasted bitter on her tongue as she shoved his hands away and picked up her bike.

His eyes helped with misunderstanding as he observed her, when he had tried to lift her bike up for her, she had only pushed his hands away again and glared. She wanted to be as far away from him and the moment as she could get.

Big Willy had watched her walk away, her steps uneven as she limped, her bike being wheeled beside her. Her posture held a darkness to it, a new layer that had never touched her porcelain cheeks before.

"What had you thought," I asked him, much older than I was at the time it happened, my feet swinging back and forth.

"Nothin' really." He smiled at me. Always smiling. "She was scared and hurt, I thought she didn't want anyone around her."

I had looked at him then, older than he ought to be but still so young. Still so little that could trouble him. Did he really understand? I often thought he didn't, he never pondered the world away like I did. He was never as unhappy as I was.

As the memory faded from her mind and she was sitting in her bedroom, Charlie was overcome with a cold realization. He had been protecting her. Big Willy had been the *savior* she was praying for and now. What would happen to him?

Her cheeks were wet, from the tears of the memory or the absolute tragedy she had struck on a person's life she didn't know. What had she done? *How* could she have done this?

"That feeling never goes away." Her lips had become dry and pale with the amount of times she had licked them, "The guilt of what you have done. Of what you could have prevented."

Her hand covered her mouth as she tried to stifle her sobs. None of this should have ever happened and Big Willy, sweet, gentle, Big Willy never should have been the one to take the blame. A person as ever loving as him should never be tainted by the actions of others.

If she had just spoken sooner, if she had just *thought* for a second.

Charlie didn't realize how loudly she had been crying, not until the door to her bedroom was pushed open and Miss Beth stepped inside, concern heavy on her face. She took one look at the girl and startled, not understanding why the young thing was so distraught or hysterical and unsure what to do to help.

"Goodness me child, whatever is the matter?" Miss Beth said as she walked toward Charlie, closing the door behind her as she did.

"It's all my fault!" The girl sobbed, rushing into the arms of the woman who had always felt so beautifully of home to the young girl. She pressed her face into the warmth of the woman's chest, her sobs choking and making it difficult for her to breathe.

Miss Beth rubs her back, unsure of the cause of the sudden immense and burning breakdown pouring through the young girl but wanting her to calm down. Either so they can fix the problem together or so that she can go and make a cup of tea.

Her warm, fleshy fingers rub circles on her back and she says, "You gotta calm down child, I can't help ya if I don't know what's wrong."

Charlie takes great heaving breaths as she tries to regain control on her vocal cords, so that she can get the words out, so that she can break through and get it all out and into the open. Her throat throbs with her almost screaming cries that had left her but she needs to say it. She has to get it all out, or it will fester and rot inside of her.

"I did something terr-terrible." She stutters out.

"What did you do child?" Miss Beth asks her, unable to believe that sweet, angelic Charlie could ever do something so terrible it would send her into such a state.

"I hurt him, Miss Beth," She cries again, "I hurt Bi Willy."

In staggered sentences with large tears flowing freely from her eyes, Charlie tells Miss Beth everything that happened. She leaves out no detail as she confesses to the horrible memory and confesses to the terrible things that had been done.

Miss Beth listens and holds the poor girl the entire time, with horror and fury winding tighter and tighter in her chest. She knew what had happened to the girl, had seen the story told in the marks that had littered her body in the aftermath but that didn't make it any easier to stomach or hear. That didn't mean that the woman wasn't horrified that someone ever had to live through that. Especially someone so young.

The bruises can fade from Charlie's body but those kinds of wounds never truly heal. The ones done to your heart and your mind.

The older woman listens, taking in each word with great care. She will have to relay this all back to the girl's mother once this is over and the girl finally gets some sleep. Real sleep, not the sweat-filled tossing and turning she has been subject to for the weeks gone by.

And when the story is over, it is Miss Beth who takes over the speech, wiping the tears from Charlie's cheeks with a wet cloth and saying the same thing over and over. "Shhh, it's not your fault girl, it's not your fault."

As the words repeat through the air like a prayer, the young girl is guided into her bed, the thin blanket tucked over her body to make her feel secure but not overheat her in the intensity of the summer.

As the older woman steps out of the room closing the door silently behind her, although nothing will wake Charlie from the exhaustion coma she had slipped into that she is sure of, it is a responding sense of justice and anger.

Those two boys will not know what was coming for them. Miss Beth hopes some kind of force will strike them down, she will pray to every god and saint there is for that to happen.

She walked down the stairs, looking for the girl's mother. This was not going to be an easy conversation. Mary Abigail Pickney was where she always was at this time of the evening Sitting in a chair by the bay window, soaking up the orange afternoon light and reading. The light was soft on her features, so undisturbed by the world.

"Mary, Ma'am," Miss Beth began, "Charlie remembered what happened."

Chapter 10:

The Truth We Tell

On Monday morning after a restless night, I work to the sound of raindrops on the roof. There is nothing quite like the sounds of rain hitting corrugated iron. It makes the rain feel so really and so connected to music. A melodic drip that reminds me so deeply of my childhood it is difficult to explain to anyone who has not experienced it.

I woke up with a stuffy head and the inklings of sickness curling around me. A stinging throat, a blocked nose and an all out pain in my body that made me feel like I would never be right again.

I lay there as the darkness slowly seeped into a gray light that slipped between the cracks and made me pull the blankets tighter around me, trying to trap a little more warmth to my body.

The rain was a good sign mama would say. The end of a drought, the wet season coming in fast to water and replenish the land. Summer was not always dry but that year it had been. A dry heat that made everyone worry about the cotton and what it meant for all of us.

I didn't move from my cocoon, not when I heard Mama and father begin to move about outside my room. Not when I knew they were expecting me to be there and would come and get me soon. Still I remained as the door was pushed in so Mama could scold me for not getting out of bed.

But as she stepped into the room she held her tongue and just looked at me. Lying there on my back staring at the ceiling with red rimmed eyes and hollowed out cheeks. For the first time in a long time, she was reminded that I was nothing more than a child. Still so small and young and only just beginning to understand and grasp onto the world. My youth was slipping away from me faster than I could hold on and there was no way for me to keep track of it all. No way for me to stop the drip of it.

She wished there, watching me as I curled tighter into the blankets and tried to stop from shivering, that she had been able to give me a childhood without work. One in which play was always near and I was never wondering when it would be my turn to take over the burden of my family. One in which I acted my age and never knew too much.

So told me that many years later, it was her biggest regret I believe. One that I had not been able to reassure.

She didn't say anything, didn't force me to get up. Just turned around and went back into the kitchen but left the door open so she could keep an eye on me.

I fell into a hazy sleep, one in which I was unsure if I was truly awake or not. When I woke again, I was being carried by my father and placed in a bundle of blankets near the stove. Mama used to do it for us when we were much younger and got sick, to keep us warm and alive in the brutal winter. Wrapped us tight in all the warm things that we owned and set us near the fire to burn our fevers out.

The nostalgia of it all, the reminder of my youth, nearly made me start crying again. I felt so young at that moment, mama's cool hand on my cheek and father watching from the door. Trying to decide whether he should stay or go. So young and yet far too old for my body.

Mama stayed home with me, spooning warm soup into my mouth and whispering soft words to me.

"You've done so well, Sweet girl, worked so hard, just rest now." She breathed, her hand brushing through my hair as she pulled the blankets tighter around me. I did cry then, but these tears were cold against my flushed skin. She shushed me and sang me a soft lullaby from so long ago I remembered it in my body.

I did rest then, in hazy fits that I awoke to with a dry throat and aching body. Nothing felt right. I would call for Mama and she always came, helping me to drink water slowly and bringing me more soup when I could stomach it.

In the early afternoon I fell into a deep and hard sleep. Dropping out of my haze and tumbling straight into intense, wild dreams where I ran free and was trapped all at the same time. The colors and sounds are too bright to stomach and nothing really makes sense. Especially not when I woke up to my father reading the newspaper at the table and Mama making dinner. It was late judging by the fading light through the window.

I was vaguely aware that I had let Mrs. Fields down but could not seem to dwell on it for too long as I picked up my body and went to sit with father at the table with blankets still wrapped around my form. He smiled at me but didn't say anything and I appreciated it. I watched Mama cook and felt for the first time that maybe, just maybe everything would be okay. So long as I kept these moments close, Mama and father and me.

There came a knock at the door and I couldn't bear to break the feeling of rightness when I had been without it for so long now. I kept my eyes on Mama as Father stood and went to open the door.

"Good evening, Tobias," A familiar voice broke my peace but this time it was not laced with so much malice.

"Good evening Archibald." I turned to watch out of a sense of curiosity that was coming over me.

The man standing at our door was very different from the one before, he seemed small and shrunken in his body. I didn't know him that well but I would almost say that he looked guilty.

He took his hat off his head and almost bowed before my father.

"I need to speak with you and I would prefer to do it inside." For a long moment my father didn't move, looking at the man before him like he was looking for something very specific that he needed to make his decision about what he was going to do. And then he spoke, his voice in control, "I have a very ill daughter inside, make sure that you keep your voice down so as to not upset her."

The man nodded, clearly hearing the warning and knowing that right now, at this moment he was not in control of the situation.

My father stepped aside to let him inside our home and I found myself pulling tighter into myself, curling my knees up onto the chair and holding myself as small as I felt on the inside.

Archibald greeted my mother softly and all she did was nod at him before he took a seat across from me but turned to face my father. I could see the side of his face and I appreciated that he didn't try to talk to me. Just focused on the matter at hand that he came to deal with.

"I understand that you are less than inclined to have me in your home at this current moment," He began to speak, resting his hat on the table, "but I wanted to apologize for my behavior the other night. It was unacceptable."

My father nodded but did not respond. Fully giving him the space to explain himself before he made a judgment.

"I'm sure you understand that we are very protective over our daughters. When Charlie was attacked I couldn't think of anything except making it right."

He sighed and ran a hand down his face, he looked tired. "I know now that nothing could ever truly make it right, I wasn't there to protect her. I couldn't stop her from being hurt and now I have to live with the consequences."

"Your William," I watched as tears slipped down his cheeks, his voice catching in the back of his throat, "He saved her. He protected her not because he had to but because it was the right thing to do. And what did I do to repay him? I made a villain out of him and all his family."

A sob broke through the air, he was struggling to collect himself but I could tell that he needed to get it all out.

"I am so sorry. I am so sorry. He was such a good boy, such a hard worker. I know he never would have done this. It didn't make sense, it's not in the boy's nature and yet someone gave me a person to blame so I blamed them. I blamed him and now everything is a mess. I don't know how to fix it except to say that I am sorry."

I looked at him for a long time, as the room drew silent and cold. This man sitting in front of me was just as lost and emotional as the children that I played with. Just as unknowing as I was. I was startled by the realization that adults could be children too. Emotional, irrational and acting on their instincts. Perhaps you only grow up for certain things.

"I am not sure if I can forgive you Archibald," He choked back a sob at my father's words, "My family has given a lot to you and you were not even willing to hear us out. You did the one thing I never thought you would, you judged us for our skin first."

The man nodded his head and broke out into a flurry of *"I am sorry."*

"My son may never be able to return, it might never be safe for him and yet you go on as you were." My father added and Archibald nodded his head.

"I know."

"Did you find who it was that attacked Charlie?"

Archibald took a breath before speaking, "We did. But it's a sensitive matter. It will be up to their parents about what will be done with them but I think that it will just be swept under the rug. Quickly forgotten and brushed aside. I cannot give you anything more. It is out of my hands."

Why was it a delicate matter now? It had not been delicate when they had been so quick to blame my brother. So quick to throw him away so that they had a person to blame. Why was it not being swept under the rug when it had been one of us. They were so willing to protect their own and burn the rest of the world if they had to.

"William will be welcomed back of course, we would love to have him back. We will up your shares in the plantation; it is the least that we can do. Perhaps we can even get him a paying job in the house."

My father listened to him with an expressionless face, just taking in his words with nods and hums. Archibald didn't understand, of course he couldn't, he had always been the one in power. He would never understand the damage. The horror that had been done to not just our but all the residents of Black Town's lives. What we had to go through and will still have to go through as we earn our place back in society. As we fight to be seen as human once more.

I could see the anger in my father, the disbelief of how careless his man had been with the lives and livelihoods of so many people. When he was calmer, the wound not so fresh, he would use this guilt in order to negotiate a better life for us. To get us to benefit from it as much as we could. A small form of retribution. But right now he just sat and let the man cry. He had so many emotions for the actions he had caused. It surprised me that he felt he was entitled to our pain.

Charlie would never gain justice because of this delicate matter, and that thought made a bout of nausea and fever return. I clutched my stomach and swayed on my seat.

Eddie and Tubby would be written off as bad seeds, another terrible thing that they did that no one could fix or correct. It was just the way that it was. They came from a powerful family that would never let such an instance drag their name down. So the boys would get a tap on the wrist at most and then they would move on. Only to keep repeating the same actions over again.

"Thank you for coming to tell us, I will have a proper meeting about this all soon." My father stood and Archibald followed, "but as you can see my daughter is unwell and it is time that you leave."

Archibald made for the door and stepped outside but just before he could close it behind him my father called to him, "Just so I know, who was it that attacked Charlie?"

The man froze for a long time, like he couldn't get the words out but finally he said, "Edward Rutledge and Thomas Drayton." The door closing felt damning.

The house was silent and then Mama spoke, "Such rotten seeds those two."

I wanted to laugh, maybe cry, but instead I leaned over my chair and threw up on the floor.

***

I only realized it two days later while eating lunch. My fever had broken and I was finally feeling like myself once again. Still tired and in need of a lot more rest but not like the word was slurring around the edges from my sickness.

I had just finished eating my bread, the first real solid food Mama had allowed me when the realization had dawned suddenly.

Edward Rutledge and the dark gray eyes looking at me over a cup.

I was up and out of the house in an instant, ignoring the calls from Mama asking me where I was going. I didn't look back, just ran faster than I ever had before.

The trip to Roswell had never been so swift before. Faster than I thought was possible I was trotting up the stairs to Mrs. Fields house and throwing the door open.

I found her in the sitting room, quietly reading with a cup of tea. She was startled when I entered. I was breathing heavily and knew I looked like a disaster but at the moment I didn't care.

"You knew." I spat out, my body not able to get enough air in as I stared at the woman looking at me with such alarm and confusion. "The second you saw those scratches on Edward Rutledge's neck." I breathe, "You knew."

It takes her a moment but realization settles on her face but with a bitter smile and a softness that I am unfamiliar with in her eyes.

"I did." She admits.

"Why the hell did you not say anything?" I say not caring for my formalities, manners can be damned in his moment, " Why did you not speak up?"

She sighs, closing her book and setting it on her lap, "No one would ever take the word of the town gossip."

"This wasn't gossip!" I yell, my voice getting all pitchy as my skin starts to feel hot. " This was life. Real life. My life! This was my life and you let it burn to the ground."

If it hadn't been such an intense moment I think she might have rolled her eyes at my dramatics. I know I do when I look back on this moment.

"I think that is quite dramatic enough, Child." She spoke sternly but withheld the eyeroll for my emotional fragility. Patting the seat next to her, I hesitated before going and sitting down.

"The only person who would ever be able to clear William Johnson's name would be Charlie. Only her." She states, her eyes looking at me with conviction and wisdom. Still I want to deny it.

"But people listen to you!" I am desperate to change a past that is already so set in stone.

"Only when I have evidence," She shakes her head, "Otherwise it is merely gossip and hearsay."

"You had evidence, the scratches." I mutter, feeling less confident of what I had run all the way here to declare.

"There are other things to justify those scratches." I know she is right, I don't want her to be but I know that she is.

"It was evidence."

"Not enough." She says as she smiles at me, a look I cannot begin to describe, maybe love, "Not enough."

I deflate completely at that. My body feels all feverish again and I know I have just busted my recovering my coming all the way here but I can't really think all that hard about it.

"Oh sweet child," She whispers to me, "You cannot change the past no matter how much you try. Knowledge only comes with time."

I bite my lip hard to stop myself from crying, I feel that I have cried so much and I am tired of it. I need a break from it.

I lean back into the cushions and let my eyes close. I vaguely hear Mrs. Fields calling Petunia to bring me something cool to drink.

When it comes it comes with a wet cloth that is draped over the back of my neck as the young woman softly helps me drink, muttering about how I have only made myself sick by getting out of bed so early.

The peace in the house startled once more when the door flies open and Mama comes baring in.

"Are you out of your mind Ruby Johnson? Running out when you are barely even well? You are going to make yourself sick again and you have already taken so much time off of work and school. I thought you had some sense Child!" I take the scolding with nods and sighs. I am feeling too tired and too unwell to do much else at this moment. I just take it.

Mrs. Fields brings Mama a cup of tea and as I lie in a new haze of fever, they use the time to catch up. Apparently Petunia is gone to fetch someone to help mama and I get home. Anyone with half an eye can see that I will not be able to make the trip back.

I am not sure how we will get back home, the fever taking me again with vigor and I let it, content to fall back into my haze if it means I can rest and not think so much about everything.

***

It takes me nearly a week to recover after my runaway trip to Roswell but when I am finally properly on the mend with no signs of slip ups my parents make the decision to make the journey to see Big Willy.

Mama had dressed me in my best clothes, helping me to pull them onto my body even though I had assured her that I was old enough to do it herself.

"Let Mama help you Ruby, you're still recovering," She had said as she pulled my night dress from my body.

Once the dress was situated on my body, she took me to the table to do my hair and I had given her the bow I had carefully stashed in my room for safe keeping.

"Where did you get this?" She had asked me as she tugged my hair so that it would listen to her.

"From a friend," I replied.

It was a very long walk, about seven hours and the furthest I had ever been from Black Town.

The air is cold as we leave early in the morning, winter is clearly here but it seems to be mild after the terrible summer. We walked from before the sun was up and into the midday heat which was more of a relief than anything else. It eased off any of the cold and sat at a comfortable level making the walk easier to enjoy.

I didn't know where we were going, not even the direction. It had been so dark when we left and I followed behind my parents. I was sure that we hadn't walked through Roswell and then could only assume that we had gone in the other direction, further south.

The grass grew longer and wilder the further we walked, an area of unfarmed land that was left to do as it wished. I am sure it would be pretty in the spring when all the flowers bloom and the fields would be covered in colors but right now it is bare. Winter had stopped the plants of their colors and life and everything was dry and an ugly shade of brown.

I saw the house before my parents pointed it out and I knew that it was where we were going.

It was a little cottage seemingly in the middle of nowhere. It was a nice house that reminded me of the children's stories I had read in Mrs. Fields' house about cottages in the woods where magic happened.

The area around the house was farmed but not for any sort of commercial purposes. It was large enough to be for more than one person but small enough to not really have yield that you could sell.

We made our way past a gate and into the property where a dog greeted us, barking loudly and nodding our toes. I looked around trying to find something to connect to my brother but I couldn't see him or any sign of him.

"Yes old boy, we're here," Mama greeted as she leaned down to pet the dog and then kept walking. I followed behind her.

When we rounded the corner was when I first saw him. My brother, William.

The first thing that struck about seeing him again after so long was how small he seemed to be. He didn't feel overwhelmingly tall or towering over me like this unyielding rock. He seemed much smaller and younger too. Like overnight he had become my little brother and I was his older sister now.

He had definitely lost weight, his cheeks a little more sunken in and his shoulders smaller and less defined. But there was something else about him. Something so different I found myself studying him to try and find out what it was.

"Willy?" Mama called to him and he turned around. His face showed all his surprise that faded softly like melting ice into joy.

He rushed toward us, hugging Mama tight, shaking Father's hand and then picking me up into a tight embrace and spinning me around.

The world whirled into colors and I clung to him because even despite his changed form, I had still missed him more than anything. My anger and sadness over his disappearance slipped off my body like shedding my clothes. I never wanted to let him go. With all of us here now, it felt like we were coming home after a very long time.

After the reunion, we went inside to have some tea and bread and speak with the woman that Willy had been staying with.

She was a strange lady that wore even stranger clothes but the tea that she gave me was sweet and so I couldn't complain much. She gave us bread with molasses and asked us about the journey.

Mama and father did most of the talking, chatting about the farm and the yield, the rain and how the walk had been.

"We would 'ave come earlier," Mama said when there was a lull in the conversation, "But Ruby got sick and took a while to get better." She gave me a look at her last words, the blame for my long recovery placed on me. I hid my smile behind my tea cup. I didn't regret running all the way to Roswell. It meant that I hadn't just stirred in my resentment for Mrs. Fields not saying anything.

I also was kind of grateful I went, Mrs. Fields sent her good biscuits with Petunia as a well wish of my recovery. I would do it all again if it meant I got biscuits.

"Good to see that she had recovered well then" The woman said, I had missed her name and felt too embarrassed to ask for it again.

"Willy," My father addresses, "Your name has been cleared."

The room was silent for a moment before Willy was nodding with a smile on his lips.

"The Pickney girl remembered what happened and told her parents." Mama added resting a hand on his arm.

"So," He began, looking around the table with hopeful eyes, "Can I come back home?"

Mama and Father looked at each other before speaking, "Not just yet."

He seemed to fall back into his melancholy at her words, "It's just not safe, people are still determined to take it out on us even though the truth has been revealed. We just need some time to make sure it will be safe for you to come home."

"Oh," is all he says.

"You are welcome to stay for as long as you need, Willy," The woman says. "My home will always be open to you and with my back these days I love having you around. The extra hands are needed."

"Thank you, Ma'am," He says but I can still see he is disappointed. He thought we would be coming to bring him home but even I can see that it is a bad idea. I don't know when he will be able to come back but until the Whites start seeing the Blacks as people again it's not going to be safe for him.

I watch him for a moment and then I come to the realization that maybe he is not the one that has changed. Maybe this is the exact same Willy that walked out of Black Town all those months ago.

I almost can't believe how he is not as changed and different as I but he seems to be almost identical.

Maybe a little softer and a little sadder but still the same Willy.

It is I who is so changed and different. So molded and shaped but the fire that burnt hot and hard around me. I had become completely different that I cannot recognize the people around me as they have not changed in the ways that I have.

The younger my brother seems, the older and older I grow.

We finish our bread and tea and Willy takes me out to show me the work he has been doing. Telling me all about the new plants he has learned about and how to take care of him. He shows me the beautiful patterns he built in the soil and how much better they have been going since Martha, that's the woman's name, has had someone around to do the heavy lifting.

In return I tell him about my own garden that I built in Roswell, I tell him about the flowers that will bloom in the spring and all the things I had to clear just so I could replant them. He seems interested but doesn't know much about gardens of beauty and practicality.

I want to tell him how it was his hands that guided it's growth, his shadow looming over me that made me do it but I simply can't.

His experience of this all is so different to mine, he built fields of fruit while I was wiping spit from my face and trying not to get tripped on the way home.

I lived in anger and hate while he flourished in a quiet place far from it all, he simply would not be able to understand any of it. The pain and burn of our existence in his absence would only hurt him.

So instead, for the first time in my time, I don't. I don't tell my brother about everything that happened while he was away when I used to tell him everything. I tell him about my garden and I tell him about being sick but nothing else.

He has been safe from it all, he will remain that way.

And the rest of us will pick up the pieces and try to find a way to live, try to find a way to move past it into the next summer and all the ones that follow. We know how deeply the world burns but we also know how to heal them. We know so much more than we should. Humanity always shows its ugliest parts before it shows its beauty.

The sunset here looks different and I watch it go down with a complete family and heart too big and too small for my chest.

Epilogue

The dust in the church hung suspended in the air. It had been stirred up and swirled around the room by all the words that had been pulled from the woman's mouth. The midmorning sun had sagged under the weight of day and it would be dark soon. An inkiness already creeping onto the horizon.

The two strangers did not move when the story came to an end. Could not speak for fear of breaking the spell that had wrapped around them so tightly and beautifully.

There had been so many things said in the story that the man had to process and digest and yet he still found himself being greedy for more. Her words were too much but too little, there was still so much left unsaid and so many questions he wanted answered.

But he could also feel it, how their time was slowly coming to an end, soon he would outstay his welcome and so his chance to question and know more was limited. He could afford a few but only that.

"He really was a good man," he finally spoke and tipped his head to the casket.

"Yes," the woman smiled. "He was."

"Did Big Willy live a good life in the end?" He also asked, if he could not ask for details and everything else that he was desperate to know then at least he could ask this.

"A hard life," she responded softly. "Hardship and work was a common occurrence in his days but he was happy and surrounded by people who loved him. In the end that has to be something. Happiness is often such a rare commodity."

He nodded his head, so many lived lives that were considered good but very few were happy and content with them. He couldn't say that he was happy for large portions of his life but at least now, at the end, he had worked it out.

"That's good to hear, that he found peace. Did he ever go back to Black Town?" He wanted to know this one a little more than the others, it seemed so very important to it all, such a vital detail in the story.

"Yes, but many years later. He didn't stay long." Her fingers smoothed the bow on her hat, making sure that the material was clean and neat, "He had made a life for himself elsewhere at that point, Black Town was more of a memory of home than it was an actual one."

How funny that one moment completely resets the course of your life. Never to return to its previous path.

"Did anything ever happen to Eddie and Tubby?" At that question she signed, a deep one that came right from the very depths of her soul.

"I don't know, I don't think so. I heard through this and that they were removed from their family. They didn't inherit anything from their parents and were disowned." She thought for a moment and then kept speaking, "Someone told me many years after it all ended that Eddie had wound up in jail someplace else, but I am not sure if it's true. Supposedly, Tubby lived a simple life and didn't get into trouble after he parted ways with Eddie. But no, they never received any repercussions for what they did to Charlie."

"And Ruby," He asked his last question, the sun was only just peeking over the windows now. It was time to leave. "Did Ruby live the life she wanted?"

"No," says the woman before a found smile pulled across her features. "But she lived the one she needed."

Unsure of what that meant, he sat up and turned to her.

"I want to thank you for your time and the story. I only wish I had heard it when I was younger," he smiled politely.

When she smiled back it lit up her whole face and he could see the young girl within her.

"It was my pleasure, I hope that it was helpful to you in some way. Even if it wasn't, everyone loves a good story," she laughed and it filled the Church up with its warmth and brightness.

He stood to leave and shook her hand. He had paid his respects and it was time he went on his way. He took two steps down the aisle and then stopped and turned to the woman.

"I'm sorry," he started, "I didn't catch your name."

She smiled, like she knew a very important secret that he didn't. "Ruby Johnson. It is a pleasure to meet you."

He stared at her for a long moment, taking in the woman that had lived through so much and was so tired of him without even realizing it. Then, he laughed, loud, joyful and a little hysterically. The universe has a funny way of playing games with us. Making us think that we knew how everything was going to turn out when we didn't.

"James Pickney. And the pleasure is all mine."

She smiled at him, again, like she knew something that he didn't and he smiled back. The air around them held steady. So much of their lives had been impacted, changed and built by the other. Both of them had just been observers in the events, watched it all happen to everyone around them without knowing how to stop it and being forever changed by it.

"How is your sister?" Ruby asks, a new warmth between them.

"Old," he laughs. "But still vibrant in her old age."

Ruby nodded. She could see the truth in that. The bright and kind young girl being a fiery old woman that didn't take anything from anyone. Once you lost as much as she had, you learned to keep what was still close to your chest safe and protected.

"Thank you." She speaks once more, "for coming to Big Willy's funeral. It means a lot to me and our family that you are here."

He nodded his head, and then sighed, "I cannot change what happened but the very least that I could do was recognize that he was a great man."

Ruby nodded at his words, "that he was."

"You know, Ruby, you also didn't deserve this. No child should have to grow up that quickly."

"I am a product of my town, James. I would have had to grow up sooner rather than later anyway. But still, thank you."

They look at each other for a moment longer but when the light dims from the setting sun, James tips his hat to Ruby then walks out of the church.

He will not take her grieving from her any longer. Now is her time to remember her brother and the happy parts of their life together, not the sorrow that nearly took their family from them.

At the very least they deserve that. A peaceful ending.

Made in the USA
Columbia, SC
31 May 2023